JUST DISGUST

Is this the right book f...
Take the DISGUSTING TES...

YES	NO	
☐	☒	Do you ever pick your nose?
☒	☒	Do you ever talk in burps?
☐	☒	Do you ever wear the same underwear two (or more) days in a row?
☐	☒	Do you ever puke so hard it comes out your nose?
☒	☐	Do you wish you knew the most disgusting word in the world?

SCORE: Give yourself one point for every YES answer.

3–5   You are completely and utterly disgusting.
       You will love this book.

1–2   You are fairly disgusting.
       You will love this book.

0   You are a disgusting liar.
       You will love this book.

Also by Andy Griffiths

Just Annoying!
Just Joking!
Just Stupid!
Just Crazy!
The Day My Butt Went Psycho!
Zombie Butts from Uranus!

JUST DISGUSTING!

ANDY GRIFFITHS

with illustrations by
TERRY DENTON

Scholastic Inc.

New York   Toronto   London   Auckland   Sydney
Mexico City   New Delhi   Hong Kong   Buenos Aires

JUST DISGUSTING!

ISBN 0-439-54954-X

Text copyright © 2002 by Backyard Stories Pty. Ltd.
Illustrations copyright © 2002 by Terry Denton

12 11 10 9 8 7 6 5 4 3   5 6 7 8 9 10/0

Printed in the U.S.A.   40
First Scholastic printing, February 2005

CONTENTS

101 REALLY
Disgusting
THINGS

1. Brussels sprouts.

2. Maggots.

3. Brussels sprouts with maggots in them.

4. Picking your nose.

5. Picking your nose and eating it.

6. Picking somebody else's nose and eating it.

7. Scabs.

8. Scabs with maggots.

9. Maggots with scabs.

10. Shower-drain hair.

11. The slimy stuff that comes out of the shower drain when you pull on the shower-drain hair.

12. Animals that get squashed in the middle of the road and then get run over a whole lot of times until they're just disgusting red blobs.

13. Dog poo.

14. Accidentally stepping in dog poo and getting it on the bottom of your shoe.

15. Getting dog poo on your fingers when you're trying to get the dog poo off the bottom of your shoe.

16. Eating a hot dog and thinking that it tastes like dog poo and then realizing that it's probably because you forgot to wash your hands after trying to get the dog poo off the bottom of your shoe.

17. Bad breath.

QUACK QUACK!

2

18. Cockroaches.

19. Headless cockroaches. (Disgusting true fact #1: Cockroaches can live for nine days without their heads.)

20. Headless cockroaches with maggots coming out of the holes where their heads used to be.

21. People who stay in the swimming pool all day long and don't get out, not even to go to the bathroom.

22. The story about the woman who went to Africa and came back with a mysterious lump that kept moving all around her body and then one day the lump was gone but her eyes were really itchy and she looked in the mirror and there were all these tiny white baby spiders coming out of her eyes.

23. Danny's handkerchief. It hasn't been washed for two and a half years. Makes a cracking sound when unfolded.

24. Dirty undies.

25. Your guts. (Disgusting true fact #2: If you took your guts out of your stomach and stretched them out, you would have enough to circle a soccer field three and a half times.)

26. When some stupid old song from the last century comes on the radio and your parents start dancing and kissing right in front of you.

27. Zombies.

28. Flesh-eating zombies.

29. Flesh-eating zombies with really bad breath because they forgot to clean their teeth after feasting.

30. Ear wax.

31. Dirty diapers.

32. Blood clots.

33. Collecting your blood clots in an old jam jar and using them to make red paint.

34. Eating a piece of toast with jam and thinking that it tastes a little bit like toast with blood clots and then realizing that it's probably because you accidentally put the jam jar full of blood clots back into the pantry instead of your paint box.

35. *#@!#@%$! (Disgusting true fact #3: "*#@!#@%$!" is the most disgusting word in the English language. In fact, the word is so disgusting that anybody who hears it immediately throws up and their head explodes. If you really want to know what the word is, ask your teacher. If you throw up and your head explodes, you'll know they told you the truth.)

36. Spit.

37. A whole cup of spit.

38. Drinking a cup of cold water and realizing that you just drank a cup of cold spit by mistake.

39. Sniffing one end of a strand of spaghetti up your nose.

40. Coughing up the other end of the strand of spaghetti and letting it hang out of your mouth.

41. Grabbing one end of the strand of spaghetti with one hand and the other end of the spaghetti in your other hand and sliding it back and forth.

42. Pulling the strand of spaghetti out of your nose and eating it.

43. Pulling a strand of spaghetti out of some-body else's nose and eating it.

44. Puke.

45. Sooty's puke.

46. Sooty eating his puke.

47. Sooty re-puking his puke.

48. Sooty re-eating the re-puked puke he just puked, etc., etc., etc.

49. Puke with maggots in it.

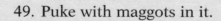

50. When you puke so hard that it comes out of your nose.

51. When you break an egg and it's got blood in it.

52. When you break an egg and it's got blood and a half-formed chicken in it.

53. When the half-formed chicken drags its mutant body across the bloody plate toward you saying, "Mama . . . Mama . . ."

54. Slugs.

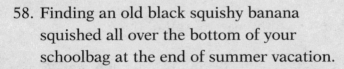

55. Really big fat slimy slugs.

56. A really big fat slimy slug doing a striptease.

57. Old black squishy bananas.

58. Finding an old black squishy banana squished all over the bottom of your schoolbag at the end of summer vacation.

59. Finding a broken egg in the bottom of your schoolbag at the end of vacation and

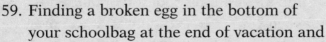

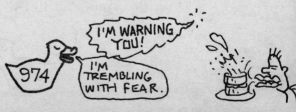

I'M WARNING YOU!

I'M TREMBLING WITH FEAR.

974

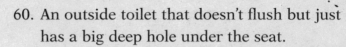

there's a half-formed chicken dragging its
mutant body around saying, "Mama . . .
Mama . . ."

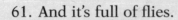

60. An outside toilet that doesn't flush but just
has a big deep hole under the seat.

61. And it's full of flies.

62. And maggots.

63. Dropping your new watch into the big
deep hole in an outhouse, and while you're
trying to get it out you lean over a little bit
too far and you fall in, and you can't yell
for help because the flies and maggots fill
up your mouth, and you can't get them out
because you're too busy trying to keep
yourself afloat.

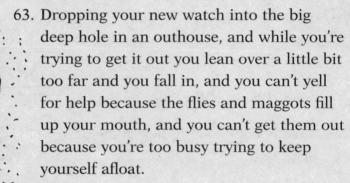

64. Pus.

65. A swimming pool full of pus.

66. Accidentally dropping your new watch
into a swimming pool full of pus, and
when you try to get it out you lean over a
little bit too far and you fall in, and you

can't yell for help because the maggots fill up your mouth, and you can't get them out because you're too busy trying to keep yourself afloat.

67. I think I forgot to mention that there are maggots in the swimming pool full of pus. But there are. **THERE ARE MAGGOTS IN THE PUS!!!**

68. Biting into an apple and finding a worm.

69. Biting into an apple and finding half a worm.

70. Biting into an apple and finding a headless cockroach.

71. Biting into an apple and realizing that it wasn't an apple at all — it was just a big wet bloodstained furball that your cat coughed up into the fruit bowl that morning.

72. Realizing that you're following your cat around hoping that it will cough up another big wet bloodstained furball

because you liked the taste of the first one so much.

73. Spiders.

74. Spiders' guts. Their stomachs contain powerful enzymes designed to liquefy everything they come into contact with.

75. Hitting a spider with a hammer and the contents of its abdomen flying out and hitting you in the eye.

76. When your eyeball liquefies and dribbles down your face and makes everybody who sees you either scream or vomit.

77. Or both.

78. Standing outside with your mouth open and a fly flies in and you're so surprised that you swallow it.

79. Standing outside and you look up and a bird poops in your eye.

80. Standing outside and you look up and a bird poops in your mouth.

81. Standing outside and you've just had a bird poop in your eye AND your mouth

UH-OHH!!

and looking down and realizing that you just stepped in dog poo. (See numbers 13–16.)

82. People who fold their eyelids back so you can see the reddish-white part underneath.

83. Burps.

84. People who can burp the alphabet, for example, Danny Pickett.

85. People who try to burp the alphabet, but try a little bit too hard and end up vomiting instead, for example, me.

86. Farts.

87. People who can fart the alphabet.

88. People who try to fart the alphabet, but try a little bit too hard. . . .

89. Lumpy milk.

90. Lumpy milk with maggots in it.

91. Only realizing that the milk is lumpy and has maggots in it when it's in your mouth.

CATE AND ANNA'S DISGUSTING DAY.

SPLAT!

THE END.

92. Only realizing that the milk is lumpy and has maggots in it after you've ACTUALLY swallowed it.

93. When you've swallowed lumpy milk with maggots in it and you puke so hard that maggots come out of your nose.

94. Puke with maggots in it. (Yes, I know this has already been on the list, but it's just SO disgusting I had to put it on again.)

95. The smell of dead fish.

96. The smell of a cat's breath after it's been eating dead fish.

97. Disgusting true fact #4: Scientific studies have shown that 90 percent of the dirt under people's fingernails is not in fact dirt — it's feces (that's the scientific name for poop). The other 10 percent is peanut butter.

98. Watching television and seeing them open up somebody's stomach and seeing the person's guts.

12

WHERE'S IT GOING?

99. Playing around with a sharp knife and accidentally opening up your OWN stomach and seeing all your OWN guts.

100. Playing around with a sharp knife and accidentally opening up your own stomach and seeing all your guts fall out of your stomach and all over the floor, and then a dog runs in and eats them and then it pukes them up and then it re-eats them and then poops, and you're just standing there with your mouth open and a fly flies in and you're so surprised that you swallow it, and then a bird comes in and poops in your eyes and you can't see anything so you're staggering around blindly clutching your throat, and you step in the dog poo and you go sliding out of control and crash down into the bathtub, which is full of pus and dead fish and scabs and brussels sprouts all bobbing around, and you pull the plug so that you don't drown but you accidentally pull the drain hair up with it, and attached to the end is a half-formed

IF THIS PAGE IS TOO DISGUSTING EVEN FOR YOU, THEN WHY NOT LEARN HOW TO KNIT A LOVE HEART?

TAKE TWO BALLS OF WOOL.

(CAT'S FUR BALLS WILL DO.)

TAKE TWO VERY LONG FROZEN MAGGOTS...

START KNITTING!

CUDDLE UP TO KNITTED LOVE HEART...

AND FEEL WONDERFUL.

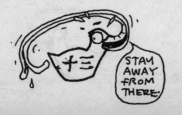

STAY AWAY FROM THERE.

mutant chicken and it's going, "Mama . . . Mama . . ." and you're so disgusted that you say, "*#@!#@%$!," forgetting that if you hear "*#@!#@%$!" your head will explode, and so your head explodes and your tongue flies into the toilet and your eyes go into a spider's web and the spider starts liquefying them, which is kind of lucky because then your mom and dad come waltzing into the bathroom smooching and kissing and they say, "Hmmm, I wonder whose body this is?" and then they start eating it because they're not really your mother and father at all — they're flesh-eating zombies, and you think things can't possibly get any more disgusting but then they DO because a big fat slug comes in and starts doing a striptease — which you can't see, but you can sense — and so your headless, gutless, half-eaten corpse runs out of the house and onto a busy road, yelling, "HELP! MY PARENTS ARE FLESH-EATING ZOMBIES AND THERE'S A SLUG DOING A STRIPTEASE IN THE BATHROOM!" but none of the cars stop

14

because nobody in their right mind would stop for a headless gutless half-eaten corpse — they just run over you . . . and over you . . . and over you until you're just this disgusting red blob in the middle of the road. Well, mostly red except for the pus and the little white bits, which are the remains of the maggots. (I think I forgot to mention that there are maggots in the pus. But there are. **THERE ARE MAGGOTS IN THE PUS!!!**)

101. This list. (See numbers 1 through 101.)

Brussels sprouts

I'm sitting at the kitchen table with Dad and Jen. Mom is serving dinner. She puts a plate down in front of me. I look at it.

Roast chicken.

Good.

Gravy.

Good.

Roast potatoes.

Good.

Brussels sprouts.

Bad.

FIVE OF THEM!

Bad. Bad. Bad. Bad. Bad.

I hate brussels sprouts.

And when I say I hate brussels sprouts, I don't just mean I hate brussels sprouts, I mean I REALLY hate brussels sprouts.

And when I say I REALLY hate brussels

sprouts, I don't just mean I REALLY hate brussels sprouts, I mean I REALLY REALLY hate brussels sprouts.

And when I say I REALLY REALLY hate brussels sprouts, I don't just mean I REALLY REALLY hate brussels sprouts, I mean I REALLY REALLY REALLY REALLY REALLY REALLY REALLY REALLY REALLY REALLY hate brussels sprouts.

Who wouldn't hate them?

They're green.

They're slimy.

They're moldy.

They're horrible.

They're putrid.

They're foul.

Apart from that, I love them.

No, I don't. That was just a joke. There's absolutely NOTHING to love about brussels sprouts. Nothing at all. They're disgusting.

And when I say brussels sprouts are disgusting, I don't just mean they're disgusting, I mean they're REALLY disgusting.

And when I say they're REALLY disgusting, I don't just mean they're REALLY disgusting, I mean they're REALLY REALLY disgusting.

I HATE BRUSSELS SPROUTS, TOO.

17

THE EVEN MORE DISGUSTING THING FROM PAGE 11...

HAS BEEN MOVED TO PAGE 97.

And when I say they're REALLY REALLY disgusting, I don't just mean they're REALLY REALLY disgusting, I mean they're REALLY REALLY REALLY REALLY REALLY REALLY REALLY REALLY REALLY REALLY REALLY disgusting.

So why did my mom have to go and spoil a perfectly good roast chicken dinner by giving me FIVE???

Surely she can't possibly expect me to EAT them.

"Come on, Andy," says Mom. "Don't just sit there looking at your dinner. Eat up."

"All of it?" I say.

"All of it!" she says firmly.

"Even the brussels sprouts?" I say.

"Even the brussels sprouts," she says.

I can't believe it. She DOES expect me to eat them.

"But I HATE brussels sprouts," I say.

"Okay," says Mom. "Suit yourself. But if you don't eat all of your brussels sprouts, you won't get any dessert."

Huh?

No dessert?

If there's one thing I love, it's dessert.

I JUST KNOW THESE WILL BE GOOD FOR YOU.

UH-OH.

And when I say I love dessert, I don't just mean I love dessert, I mean I REALLY love dessert.

And when I say I REALLY love dessert, I don't just mean I REALLY love dessert, I mean I REALLY REALLY love dessert.

And when I say I REALLY REALLY love dessert, I don't just mean I REALLY REALLY love dessert, I mean I REALLY REALLY REALLY REALLY REALLY REALLY REALLY REALLY love dessert.

And no pile of brussels sprouts is going to stop me from getting it, that's for sure.

"But that's not fair!" I say to Mom.

"Yes, it is," says Mom. "It's perfectly fair."

"If you don't eat your dinner, you don't get dessert. That's the deal," says Dad. "You know that."

Some deal. I never had a say in it. As if I'd agree to a stupid deal like that.

Jen snickers. She pokes her fork into a brussels sprout and raises it to her lips.

"Mmmmmm," she says, putting the sprout into her mouth and acting like it's the most beautiful thing she's ever tasted. "You don't know what you're missing, Andy."

19

I know she's just trying to annoy me, but it gives me an idea.

"OH NO!" I say, jumping to my feet and pointing out the kitchen window. "I DON'T BELIEVE IT!"

Mom, Dad, and Jen all jump to their feet as well.

AMAZING
BRUSSELS
SPROUT
FACTS
Nº 3487.

"What is it?" says Mom. "Is that cat back again?"

"Are the birds on my new lawn?" says Dad.

"Is it Craig?" says Jen. "But he said he wasn't coming until later! I can't let him see me like this!"

While they're all staring out of the window trying to figure out what I've seen, I take one of my sprouts and slip it onto Jen's plate. It's too easy, really.

FIRST B.S.
ON MOON:
1972

B.S. FIRST
WINS
KENTUCKY
DERBY, 1972

"Just kidding," I say, sitting back down.

Everybody else sits down as well.

Mom sighs.

Dad shakes his head.

"Are you going to be an idiot all your life?" says Jen.

1972. FIRST
B.S. TO
CLIMB MT.
EVEREST

"Probably," I say. "The pay's a little low, but the hours are good . . . and you can pretty much work whenever you want."

She ignores my reply, stabs the sprout I just put on her plate, and puts it into her mouth.

Do I feel any pity for her?

No, I do not.

MMPH...
MMPH.

20

She deserves it.

One down. Four to go.

"Excuse me, funny boy," says Dad. "Would you mind passing me the pepper?"

I look at the pepper grinder. I hate pepper. It always makes me sneeze.

Of course!

Pepper! Sneezing! The oldest trick in the book! Why didn't I think of it sooner?

"Sure," I say, quickly putting one of my brussels sprouts into my mouth.

I pick up the pepper grinder, pass it across the table to Dad, and then launch into the biggest fake sneeze in the history of big fake sneezes.

Ah . . .

I grab a tissue out of my pocket

AH . . .

I unfold it and hold it up to my face.

AH-CHOO!

I spit the brussels sprout out into my tissue, wipe my nose, and quickly put the whole thing back into my pocket.

"Bless you," says Mom.

"Thanks," I say. "I think some pepper got up my nose."

Mom nods.

Jen's still ignoring me.

Dad's grinding pepper onto his dinner.

21

I got away with it again.

I quickly shovel some chicken, gravy, and potato into my mouth to get rid of the taste of the sprout.

Two down. Three to go.

I feel something nudge my foot.

Sooty!

He's not supposed to be in the kitchen while we're eating, but he's managed to sneak in and hide underneath the table, anyway.

Which is fantastic, because Sooty eats anything.

Even brussels sprouts.

I hunch forward over my plate, conceal one of the sprouts in the palm of my hand and sneak it under the table to Sooty's waiting wet mouth.

Yes! He's eating it!

Good dog!

He'll be able to eat the other two for me as well.

Suddenly, the most disgusting, eye-watering smell fills the kitchen.

Mom looks at Dad.

Dad looks at me.

I look at Jen.

Jen looks at Mom.

We all shrug.

Dad looks under the table. "How did that dog get in here?" he says, jumping up.

AMAZING BRUSSELS SPROUT FACTS Nº 247.

THE MOON IS A BIG ALBINO B.S.

SCHUMACHER WINS GRAND PRIX USING B.S. TIRES

THE BLACK BITS ON THE END OF DOGS' NOSES ARE ACTUALLY OLD B.S.'s

Sooty shoots out from underneath the table.

Dad chases him and shoos him out the back door.

Darn.

Just when I was so close!

"I bet Andy let him in," says Jen. "He's probably been giving him food under the table."

"Yeah, right," I say. "As if."

Dad sits back down and looks at me suspiciously.

"You haven't been wasting good food on that mongrel, have you?" he says.

"No," I say.

I'm not lying, either. Whatever brussels sprouts are, they are definitely NOT good food.

I eat the rest of my dinner and try to figure out how to get rid of the two remaining sprouts.

I can't put any more on Jen's plate because she's already finished hers. She'd be sure to notice. And I can't sneeze again because my one tissue is already full. And who's going to help me now that Sooty's gone?

I know!

The X-Men.

My X-Men undies, that is.

It's going to take a little skill to do it without anybody seeing me, but I think it's possible.

VERY BIG SLUG.

IN ANSWER TO A QUESTION ASKED ON PAGE 147, IT IS A BAD IDEA!!

WHAT?

23

BOOM!

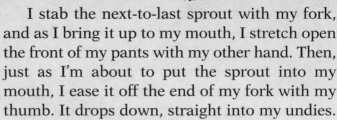

I stab the next-to-last sprout with my fork, and as I bring it up to my mouth, I stretch open the front of my pants with my other hand. Then, just as I'm about to put the sprout into my mouth, I ease it off the end of my fork with my thumb. It drops down, straight into my undies.

DO YOU KNOW HOW DANGEROUS BRUSSELS SPROUTS CAN BE?

TURN TO PAGE 30.

A direct hit!

Sure, it feels disgusting, but I'd rather have a brussels sprout squishing around in my undies than squishing around in my stomach.

Four down, one to go.

But this one's not going to be a problem.

There's a pile of chicken bones on my plate.

I can just hide it under there.

Then all I have to do is scrape the sprout off my plate and into the mulch can and the nightmare will be over.

Here goes.

"Thanks, Mom," I say, grabbing my plate and getting up. "That was delicious. I'll just clear the table."

"What?" says Jen. "You NEVER clear the table!"

"Not so fast, Andy," says Mom. "You haven't quite finished."

"What do you mean?" I say. "I've only got bones left. You can't expect me to eat bones."

"It's not the bones I'm talking about," says Mom. "It's the brussels sprout underneath them."

URP!

"What brussels sprout?" I say.

"That one there," says Mom, pointing at it.

"Oh!" I say, acting surprised. "THAT brussels sprout! I didn't see it there."

Mom tilts her head to one side and raises her eyebrows. "Do I look like I was born yesterday?" she says.

"Well, actually," I say, "you do look very young for someone so old."

"Nice try, Andy," says Mom. "Sit down and finish your dinner."

I sit down. I stare at my plate. "Do I have to eat it?" I say.

"Yes!" says Mom.

"But I can't eat any more," I say. "You gave me too many brussels sprouts."

"I gave you the same as everyone else," says Mom.

"But everyone else is bigger than me," I say. "I should get less!"

"No, you should get more," says Dad, flexing his biceps. "Don't you want to grow up to be as big and strong as me?"

"I AM big and strong," I say.

They all laugh.

"What's so funny?" I say.

"Your arms are like toothpicks and your legs are like broomsticks," says Jen. "If the wind blows too hard, you fall over. You're a WEED!"

"And you're a pig!" I say.

CAKE
WITH
BRUSSELS
SPROUTS.

"Thank you," says Jen. "You just called me a P-I-G. That stands for Pretty Intelligent Girl."

"No, it doesn't," I say. "It stands for Putrid Idiotic Geek!"

Jen gives me a look. Not a nice look, either. A Putrid Idiotic Geek look.

"Ignore him, Jen," says Dad. "Andy, just shut up and eat your sprout."

"I can't," I say. "I'm full."

"What a shame," says Mom. "You won't be able to have any dessert."

No dessert?

But I LOVE dessert!

And when I say I LOVE dessert, I don't just mean I LOVE dessert, well . . . you know what I mean. And so does Mom. She's got me in a bind.

ANSWER
TO PAGE
147.

YES!

NO!

I get the sprout out from underneath the pile of chicken bones.

It sits there.

Taunting me.

One horrible, disgusting, moldy, old, slimy, green, putrid brussels sprout. The horriblest, disgustingest, moldiest, oldest, slimiest, greenest, putridest brussels sprout of them all. And to make things even worse, it's cold.

Mom is watching me like a hawk.

So is Dad.

And Jen.

"Come on, Andy," pleads Jen. "Just hurry up

NO MORE!

XXVI

ANDY'S BRUSSELS SPROUTS.

and eat it and then we can have dessert!"

"All right, all right," I say.

There's only one thing to do. ←

I'm going to have to put it in my mouth, go to the bathroom, and spit it out. And while I'm there I'll be able to get the other one out of my undies.

I stab the sprout with my fork and hold it up in front of my face.

Have you ever looked really closely at a brussels sprout?

Well, if you haven't, I sure wouldn't recommend it.

It's horrible.

A layer of wrinkly green skin wrapped around another layer of wrinkly green skin wrapped around another layer of wrinkly green skin wrapped around another layer of — you guessed it — wrinkly green skin. And so on. And so on. And so on.

But nothing is going to stop me from getting to my dessert.

Not even a brussels sprout.

I put it in my mouth.

Yuck.

It's the most disgusting brussels sprout I've ever tasted.

The sooner I get it out of my mouth the better!

I stand up.

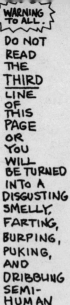

WARNING TO ALL.
DO NOT READ THE **THIRD** LINE OF THIS PAGE OR YOU WILL BE TURNED INTO A DISGUSTING SMELLY, FARTING, BURPING, PUKING, AND DRIBBLING SEMI-HUMAN BEING!!

TOO LATE!!

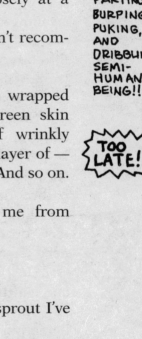

NOT FAIR

EAT US, TOO

27

"Where do you think you're going?" says Dad.

I push the brussels sprout to one side of my mouth.

"To the bathroom," I say with difficulty. It's not easy to talk with a whole brussels sprout in your mouth.

"Don't let him," says Jen. "He's not going to eat it. It's a trick! He's going to spit it out!"

"No, I'm not," I say.

"You can go to the bathroom AFTER you've swallowed the brussels sprout," says Mom.

"But I'm BURSTING!" I say. A bit of spit flies out of my mouth and lands on the table in front of Jen. It's green.

"You mean you're DISGUSTING!" says Jen.

"Swallow the sprout," says Dad. "THEN you can go to the bathroom. That's the deal."

"What kind of deal is that?" I say. "I eat a sprout, and I'm rewarded with a trip to the bathroom? Your deals are getting worse. I'm going to get myself a lawyer."

"You don't need a lawyer," says Jen. "You need a psychiatrist!"

"He'll need a doctor if he doesn't sit down and eat that brussels sprout," says Dad.

"Was that a threat?" I say, more green spit flying out of my mouth. "I'm going to call my lawyer!"

"SIT DOWN!" yell Dad, Mom, and Jen all at the same time.

I GOTTA GET OUTTA HERE.

28

NOT FAIR

I sit down.

All eyes are on me.

My escape route has been blocked.

I've got the world's most disgusting brussels sprout in my mouth and there's nothing I can do about it.

I can't flush it down the toilet.

I can't sneeze it into my handkerchief.

I can't feed it to Sooty.

I can't slip it onto Jen's plate.

I can't put it down my undies.

There's only one thing to do.

There's only one thing I CAN do.

Something I've never done before!

It's sick!

It's twisted!

It's desperate!

But I'm just sick, twisted, and desperate enough to try it.

I'm going to swallow the brussels sprout.

Yes, I'm actually going to swallow it.

That's how much I love dessert. I'm going to EAT the brussels sprout!

Hmmm.

It's not going to be easy.

In fact it's the hardest, most frightening, most demanding challenge I have ever faced in my entire life.

Because I hate brussels sprouts.

And when I say I hate brussels sprouts, I don't

BRUSSELS SPROUT WHEELS

29

just mean that I hate brussels sprouts, I mean I REALLY hate brussels sprouts.

And when I say I REALLY hate brussels sprouts, I don't just mean I REALLY hate brussels sprouts, I mean I REALLY REALLY hate brussels sprouts.

And when I say I REALLY REALLY hate brussels sprouts, I don't just mean I REALLY REALLY hate brussels sprouts, I mean I REALLY REALLY REALLY REALLY REALLY REALLY hate brussels sprouts.

But I'm going to do it.

Do it or die.

I might do it AND die, but that's how desperate I am.

Okay, here goes.

I sit up straight.

I grip the table with both hands.

I close my eyes and take a deep breath.

I take another deep breath.

And another.

And another.

I bite down.

A watery slime oozes into my mouth.

Don't think about it.

Don't think about it.

Think about nice things.

JUST
DISGUSTING
BY MAX.

HEE-
HEE.

30

NICE things.
Like sunny days . . .
and picnics . . .
and . . .
and . . .
flowers . . .
and . . .
and . . .
and . . .
rainbows . . .
I bite down again.
MORE SLIME!
MORE OOZE!
Don't think about it. Keep thinking NICE
things . . .

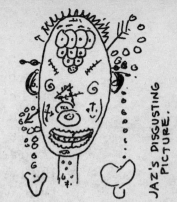

JAZ's DISGUSTING PICTURE.

   like kittens . . .
   and puppies . . .
   and ponies . . .
   and . . .
   and . . .

HELP!!

ARGH! IT'S THE BIG BAD BROCCOLI MAN!

GIANT MASHING AND PULVERIZING
MACHINES mashing and pulverizing the kittens
and puppies and ponies into blood and guts
and ooze and slime . . . green slime and . . .
no . . . no, that's not right!
That's not NICE!
It's probably safer to think about nothing
at all.
I close my eyes, put my mind in neutral,
and chew . . .

231 miles per hr!!

31

and chew . . .
and chew . . .
and chew . . .
but I can't swallow.
I can't.
I can't.
I can't do it!
But I've got to.
Otherwise, I don't get dessert.

ANDY'S
FAVORITE
DESSERT.
(small
serving)

I might miss out on something amazing . . . like Mom's chocolate sponge cake. Or . . . or maybe homemade strawberry ice cream! You've never tasted ice cream as icy or creamy or strawberry-y as my mom's homemade strawberry ice cream! Or it could be an apple pie topped with whipped cream . . . or maybe pancakes covered in maple syrup and blueberries! Or homemade chocolate ice cream! You've never tasted ice cream as icy or creamy or chocolaty as Mom's homemade chocolate ice cream! Or lemon meringue pie with the little meringue mountains on top! Or maybe it will be cheesecake . . . or raspberry tarts . . . or banana splits . . . or chocolate pudding or vanilla pudding or chocolate *and* vanilla pudding. . . .

HEY!
Wait. . . .
Something's happened. . . .
Something amazing!

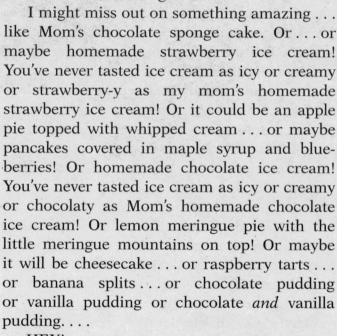

UH-OH.

My mouth is no longer full of the horriblest, disgustingest, moldiest, oldest, slimiest, greenest, putridest stuff in the world. . . .

It's gone. . . .

I must have swallowed it. . . .

I've done it!

I've really done it!

I've eaten the brussels sprout!

I can't believe it!

What an incredible achievement to have actually eaten something SO disgusting!

"Finished!" I say, opening my mouth up wide to prove that it's gone.

"Oh, gross!!!" says Jen.

"About time!" says Dad, grabbing my plate and putting it in the sink with the others.

"Good job, Andy," says Mom. "That wasn't so bad now, was it?"

I smile and nod and try not to think about what I just did. After all the trouble it took to get it down, I don't want to risk it coming back up again. I'll think about dessert instead. I close my eyes. I want it to be a surprise. Maybe tonight it will be upside-down cake . . . no, wait . . . I've got a feeling it might be pecan pie. That's my absolute favorite! No . . . banana fritters are my absolute favorite. Apart from apple crisp, of course. Mom makes a mean apple crisp. And an even meaner black forest cake. Then again, maybe

OH, NO! AN INVISIBLE WALL!!

Mom will surprise everyone and do her famous cherry pie . . . or caramel pudding . . . or maybe even — if we're really, really lucky — maybe even homemade rainbow ice cream! You've never EVER tasted ice cream as icy or creamy or rainbowy as Mom's homemade rainbow ice cream. But maybe I'm completely on the wrong track! Maybe it's chocolate fudge! Or red Jell-O! Or chocolate mousse! Or marble cake! Or Twinkies! Or . . .

I hear Dad get something out of the fridge and put it down on the table.

"Yum!" says Jen. "My favorite!"

"Mmmm," says Dad. "Delicious!"

"I just hope it was worth the wait," says Mom.

I can't stand the suspense a moment longer.

I open my eyes.

I look down at the bowl in front of me.

Oh no.

Oh no.

Oh no.

I don't believe it.

This can't be happening.

It's custard.

Cold, horrible, disgusting, moldy, old, slimy, lumpy, yellow, putrid, vomity custard.

I HATE custard. . . .

SMASH!!

34

GO TO BED!

I'm lying on the couch
reading a book[1]
when Mom comes in
and gives me THAT look.[2]

"Andy?" she says.
"Did you hear what I said?
Put down that book
and GO TO BED!"[3]

But there's no way
I'm going to bed.[4]
It's time to stall.
It's time to beg.

[1]It's really cool. It's about this kid who won't go to bed.
[2]You know the one.
[3]I did hear, but I'm pretending I didn't.
[4]I bet the X-Men don't go to bed at 8:30.

"Can't I stay up for
just half an hour more?"
"No!" says Mom,
and she points at the door.[5]

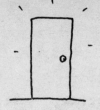

"Twenty minutes? Ten minutes?
Five minutes? One?[6]
Please can I stay up?
Please can I, Mom?"

"Come on," she says,
"Mommy knows best.
If you weren't so tired,
you wouldn't protest.[7]

[5]She thinks that just because she points at the door, I'm
going to go through it. Boy, is she in for a surprise.
[6]I've already gained at least a minute, anyway, so I'm already
winning, no matter what she says.
[7]Mom's argument makes no sense. Because if I argue,
it proves, according to her, that I'm tired and I need to
go to bed. But if I don't argue, I end up having to go to
bed, anyway.

"You've had a good time.
You've had a big day.[8]
Just be a good boy
and do what I say."

I stomp my foot
and shake my head.
"I am NOT a good boy.
I will NOT go to bed!"[9]

But then the door opens
and in walks Dad.[10]
He's got a big frown.
He looks mad.

"Not in bed yet,
Andy?" says he.
"I'll give you to
the count of three![11]

[8]Again, Mom is making no sense. No day is "bigger" or "smaller" than another. What does she think I am? An idiot?
[9]There's no way I'm going to give in. Especially since Dad's not home.
[10]Uh-oh.
[11]Dad always counts to three. I think that's because it's as high as he can count.

37

"One," he says.
He stares at me. . . .
"Two," he says.
He pauses . . . "THREE!"[12]

I leave the room.
I count to ten. . . .[13]
And then I go
back in again.[14]

"I've lost my pajamas!
I can't find my teddy![15]
I'm hungry! I'm thirsty!
I'm really not ready!"

[12]The thing is, when he says "three" he's not kidding around anymore. Better do what he says.
[13]This clearly proves that I'm smarter than my dad. It also gives him time to calm down and forget that he counted to three.
[14]You didn't really think I was going to give up that easily, did you?
[15]I'm just making this up, of course. As if I still need a teddy bear — they're just for babies.

HEE-HEE.

But Mom and Dad
ignore what I said.
"ANDY," they say,
"JUST GO TO BED!"[16]

"But I've got a sore finger
and I've got a sore butt.
I've got pains in my legs
and my arm has a cut. . . .[17]

"Not to mention my lice
and my chronic back pain.
My cloudy vision!
My aching brain![18]

"My teeth! My tongue!
My eyes! My nose!
My tonsils! My kidneys!
My stomach! My toes![19]

---

[16]Okay, they asked for it. . . .
[17]None of this is true — I'm actually 100 percent healthy, but
they don't know that.
[18]None of this is true, either — except for the lice.
[19]Actually, the more I think about it, the worse I feel.

3.142

MAKE ME.

STOP
MESSING
WITH
THE PAGE
NUMBERS!

"I can't go to sleep.
I'll wake up dead!"
"You soon will be," says Dad,
"if you DON'T go to bed!"[20]

I start to cry.[21]
I start to moan.
"How would YOU like it
up there all alone?

"How would you like it
in your lumpy old bed[22]
with the lumps in your pillow
sticking into your head?

"How would you like it
if your pajamas were too tight
and you had to lie there
with a wedgie[23] all night?"

---

[20]Did I hear right? Did my dad just give me a death threat?
That's the second time in this book, and we're only up to
page 40.
[21]Not real crying. Just pretend.
[22]My mattress is so old, it should be in a museum.
[23]I've had these X-Men pajamas since I was four. I've asked
Mom for new ones, but she says they don't make them in my
size — that they only make them for little kids. I think she's
just trying to save money.

Now Dad's really mad.
He's pretty near blowing.[24]
"All right," I say,
"I'm going! I'm going!"

I climb the stairs
toward my room.
I open the door[25]
and face my doom.

I'm all alone.
I'm full of fear.
It's cold and dark
and ghosts live here![26]

A thumping noise!
A spooky sound!
I turn around
and run back down.[27]

[24]I can tell this because he's getting bright red in the face.
[25]With difficulty. There's a huge pile of clothes on the floor.
[26]The ghosts live in my closet. That's why my clothes are all over the floor. I'm too scared to open it and put them away.
[27]I want my mommy!

OOOH, LOOK.
A NICE
ICE CREAM.

Mom looks at me.
Dad shakes his head.[28]
"I thought we told you to
GO TO BED!"

"But I'm scared," I cry,
"I heard a thump.
It came from the closet.
Something went bump![29]

"Don't make me go back there!
Don't make me stay!
It's cruelty to kids!
I'll tell the SPCA!"[30]

But Mom and Dad
don't seem too scared.[31]
"WE DON'T CARE," they shout,
"JUST GO TO BED!"

[28]My mom and dad shake their heads a lot. Especially around bedtime.
[29]It wasn't the Boogeyman, either. He lives under my bed.
[30]Society for the Prevention of Cruelty to Andys.
[31]Probably because they've heard this one before.

YUM,
YUM.

It's not looking good.
They're tough nuts to crack.
But I WILL win.
I'm NOT going back.[32]

I'm going to give it
one last try.
It's time to pull out
my ultimate lie. . . .[33]

"But I CAN'T go to bed,"
I say to those two.
"I can't go now,
I've got homework to do!"[34]

"It's too late now,"
says my dad.
"Yes," says Mom,
"it's just too bad!"[35]

---

[32]Not if I can think of another excuse, that is.
[33]I'm not saying it's good to lie, but sometimes parents leave you no choice.
[34]Well, actually, it's not a lie. I do have homework, but I have no intention of actually doing it.
[35]They obviously need a little more persuasion. Well, here it comes. . . .

I LOVE
ICE CREAM.

"But if I don't do it
I'm doomed!" I wail.
"If it's not in tomorrow
I'm going to fail![36]

"I'll be expelled!
I'll be out on the street.
Who knows what thugs
I'm likely to meet?[37]

"I'll join a gang!
I'll commit a crime![38]
I'll end up behind bars
doing time!

[36]Mom and Dad hate it when I say the F-word.
[37]I don't REALLY think any of this is going to happen, but they do.
[38]Not just walking when the sign says DON'T WALK, either. I mean a really bad crime. Like running across the road without even looking. And going to bed without brushing my teeth. And writing rap songs with lots of swears in them.

SLURP!
SLURP!

"But there isn't a jail
that could ever hold me.[39]
I'd have to break out!
I'd have to bust free![40]

"Every cop in the world
would be looking for me.
A fugitive[41]
is what I'd be.

"Hunted like an animal.
Public Enemy Number One![42]
Is that what you want
for your favorite son?"

[39]Except those ones with bars across the windows, really high walls, and razor wire around the top.
[40]You can do anything with a Swiss Army knife. Well, except for removing bars from windows, climbing really high walls, and cutting through razor wire. But besides that, practically anything.
[41]They'll probably make a movie about me and everything.
[42]Actually, the more I think about it, the more attractive it seems. It sure sounds a lot more exciting than doing homework.

I pause and wait
for my words to sink in.[43]
Have I convinced them?
Will I win?

"All right," says Dad.
"Perhaps we were wrong.
Stay up if you have to.
Stay up all night long.[44]

"Just do your homework.
Just get it all done.
We don't want you living
a life on the run."[45]

I look at my dad.
I look at my mom.
I can't believe
they've bought this one.[46]

[43]They look kind of stunned.
[44]Hmmm. This could be a trick.
[45]No, I don't think it's a trick. They've swallowed my story hook, line, and sinker.
[46]Well, I can, because I'm so brilliant. . . . I guess what I meant to say was that I can't believe that I'm so brilliant. But I am.

This is amazing!
This is great!
I got what I wanted!
I'm staying up late!⁴⁷

But then Mom and Dad
get up out of their chairs,
walk out of the room,
and start climbing the stairs.⁴⁸

"Hey, where are you going?"
I say, scratching my head.
"We're tired," says Mom.
"We're going to bed."⁴⁹

"But what about me,"
I say, "here all alone?
I'll be all by myself!
I'll be all on my own!⁵⁰

⁴⁷Wait till I tell Danny about this. He's going to be SO
jealous!
⁴⁸Huh?
⁴⁹She does look tired, actually. So does Dad. It must be awful
being that ancient.
⁵⁰Parents can be SO selfish.

"You CAN'T go to bed!
Not at THIS time of night!
You're older than me![51]
It just isn't right!"

But Dad just yawns
and says, "Good night.
Don't forget to lock up
and switch off the light."[52]

"Hey, wait!" I say,
but they've disappeared.
I don't like this —
it feels kind of weird.[53]

I'm all alone.
I'm full of fear.
I sit on the couch.
I don't like it here.[54]

[51]It doesn't make sense. The whole point of being a grown-up is that you don't have to go to bed early.
[52]This has never happened before. Never!
[53]I mean, what's their problem? Don't they LIKE spending time with me?
[54]Not anymore.

What was that noise?
I heard something squeak.[55]
Something went bump!
Something went creak!

It could be a mouse . . .
but it might be a bat![56]
No, I'm just being silly,
it's probably the cat.

But what am I thinking?
I let out a shout:
"WE DON'T HAVE A CAT!"[57]
This is creeping me out!

I try to calm down.
I turn on the TV.
But the first thing I see
is a horror movie.[58]

[55]No, it didn't come from me. Or my butt.
[56]A vampire bat that came to suck on my blood. Aaaggghhh!
[57]Well, not anymore. Not since a few years ago when Dad took
it to the vet and came home without it. He said it went to sleep.
Maybe it's finally woken up.
[58]Normally, I love horror movies, but it's not what I need
right now.

49

The living room fills
with horrible shrieks!
It's a film about ax-wielding
blood-sucking freaks.[59]

I turn it off.
I try to relax.
I take a deep breath.
But I can't get that scene out of my mind
where that poor kid who is sitting up late
all by himself watching a horror movie
suddenly has a group of blood-sucking
ax-wielding freaks jump out of the TV
and split his head open with a pickax.[60]

I get up from the couch
Like a rocket I zoom —[61]
I shoot up the stairs
and into my room!

[59]The film is called *Ax-wielding Blood-sucking Freaks*.
[60]Yes, I know this line is too long but at least it rhymes.
[61]A skyrocket that is, not a space rocket, because space rockets
are quite slow to take off at first, and I was really fast.

50

Before I know it
I'm cozy and calm
with my favorite old teddy[62]
snuggled under my arm.

I pull the blanket
up to my chin.
I'm safe[63] and I'm warm[64]
and I'm all tucked in.[65]

[62]All right, I admit it. I DO have a teddy bear. In fact, I have a few. And I like to cuddle them in bed. So what? I bet you would too if you had ghosts in your closet.

[63]A blanket, as everybody knows, is by far the best protection against ax-wielding blood-sucking freaks.

[64]They are also good for keeping you warm. Blankets, that is — not ax-wielding blood-sucking freaks.

[65]Sure, I know I didn't want to go to bed before, but I've changed my mind, okay? Give me a break. I'm overtired. I've had a big day. I'm going to sleep. Good night.

I'm no longer feeling
tense and edgy —
all I can feel
is a king-size wedgie.[66]

But I don't mind.
I'm loving this!
The lumps,[67] the thumps:[68]
it's pure bliss!

Yes . . . I know I'm in bed.
But just you wait. . . .
Tomorrow I'll stay up
REALLY late![69]

[66]Refer to footnote 23.
[67]Refer to footnote 22.
[68]Refer to footnote 26.
[69]Good night.

CaKE OF DOOM:

a chooSE your OWN baking adventure

Baking a cake: a recipe for success or a recipe for disaster? It's up to you. In this story the decisions are yours.

Your name is Andy. Tomorrow is Mother's Day and you've decided to surprise your mother by getting up early and baking her a cake. The only problem is that you've never baked a cake before. But hey, you're not going to let a minor detail like that stop you.

Good luck, happy baking, and whatever you do, BE CAREFUL!

1

Tomorrow morning has arrived. Your digital X-Men alarm clock goes off — an emergency siren, followed by the X-Men barking commands: "GET UP! TIME FOR ACTION! GO! GO! GO!"

*If you roll over and think, *I hate that clock! And I don't feel like getting up and baking a cake — I think I'll just sleep in instead . . . what has Mom ever done for me, anyway?* go to 2.
*If you jump straight out of bed and go to the kitchen, go to 3.

2

You roll over and try to shut off the alarm, but you accidentally knock over the glass of water on the nightstand. Most of the water spills onto the carpet, but some of it goes into the back of the ELECTRIC digital X-Men clock and, as you well know, water and electricity don't mix. The clock crackles and spits, the siren speeds up and slows down, the X-Men sound like they're underwater. You think *I REALLY hate that clock!* and reach over

BUMMER.

to try to turn it off again. This time you hit the clock, now alive with 220 volts of electricity, which shoots up your arm and fries your brain. Your last thought is that your mother is going to get a surprise all right — but not the one you intended. You die.

THE END

3

You go into the kitchen and you hear a strange clacking sound in the pantry. It must be one of the traps your dad set as part of his campaign against the rats that have been trying to take over the kitchen lately. They've been pooping all over the counter, pooping in the oven, pooping inside the breadbox, and your dad has declared war on them with traps, poison, and the most deadly weapon of all — your dog, Sooty. You open the door of the pantry and, sure enough, you see a rat has been caught in one of the traps. A big disgusting rat with greasy, brown, flea-ridden fur. But it's not dead — only its paw is trapped. It looks at you with its big, sad, pleading, rat eyes. You can't believe it, but you actually feel sorry for this revolting creature. . . .

*If you take the trap outside and let the rat go, go to 4.
*If you grab the big wooden rolling pin and put the rat out of its misery, go to 5.

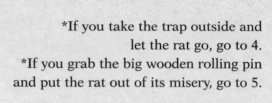

4

As you set the rat free, it turns around and bites you on the thumb, giving you a lethal dose of a deadly fast-acting form of rabies. You start frothing at the mouth. You run around in circles. You fall over. You die.

THE END

5

You bash the rat's brains out. It's a little messy. Well, actually it's more than a little messy — to tell you the truth, the rat's skull explodes like a rotten egg — but as you wipe the blood and brains off your face, you feel a

warm fuzzy inner glow that comes from knowing that you did the right thing. But as good as it feels, you can't sit around all day bashing rats' brains out. It's time to start baking that cake.

RATS BRAIN

*If you can't be bothered to bake a real cake and you reach for the box of cake mix, go to 6.
*If you can be bothered to bake a real cake and you reach for the cookbook, go to 7.

6

The box of cake mix is up on a really high shelf at the top of the pantry. You are on tiptoes reaching up for it . . . but what you don't realize is that this is where your parents have hidden your birthday present. You hardly ever go into the kitchen, and you've certainly never baked a cake before, so they thought your new bowling ball would be perfectly safe up there. You grab the packet and pull it down, but that's not all you pull down. The bowling ball drops down as well. It hits you on the head. You die.

THE END

The cookbook is up on a really high shelf at the top of the pantry. You are on tiptoes reaching up for it . . . but what you don't realize is that this is where your parents have hidden your birthday present. You hardly ever go into the kitchen and you've certainly never baked a cake before, so they thought your new bowling ball would be perfectly safe up there. You grab the cookbook and pull it down, but that's not all you pull down. The bowling ball drops down as well. It lands on the floor. "That was lucky," you say. "That bowling ball could have dropped right on top of my head. I could have died." You carry the cookbook across to the table and open it up to the section on cakes.

*If you decide to bake a carrot cake, go to 8.
*If you decide to bake a chocolate cake, go to 9.

8

The recipe calls for two cups of grated carrots. But you can't find the grater. Then you have a brainstorm. Your dad is giving

your mom a new super-powerful blender  or Mother's Day. You're sure nobody will notice if you unwrap it, use it, and then wrap it up again. So you unwrap it. There's a warning on the box that says you should read the instructions before you use it, but you never read the instructions. You're too smart. So you start putting the carrots into it. It's going pretty well but then you start wondering why the grated carrot is coming out kind of red, and then you  wonder why your fingers are hurting so much, and then you realize that it's because you didn't put the safety guard on because you didn't read the instructions, and so you've just grated all the fingers on your right hand, and you're so shocked that you fall over in a faint and all the blood in your body gushes out through your fingers all over the floor and you drown in it. You die.

THE END

You do everything that the recipe book tells you to do. You preheat the oven to 350°F. You grease and flour the bottom and sides of a 13-x-9-x-3-in. rectangular cake pan. You are then supposed to put all the ingredients into a blender. But you don't have a blender. Then you have a brainstorm. Your dad is giving your mom a new superpowerful blender for Mother's Day. You're sure nobody will notice if you unwrap it, use it, and then wrap it up again. So, you unwrap it. There's a sign on the box that says you should read the instructions before you use it, but you never read the instructions. You're too smart. So you put two cups of self-rising flour, half a teaspoon of baking soda, a quarter teaspoon of salt, half a cup of cocoa, one cup of sugar, $1\frac{1}{4}$ sticks of butter, one cup of milk, one teaspoon of vanilla extract, and two eggs into the blender and switch it on. Then you say, "Oops!" as you realize that you forgot to put the lid on the blender (which you would have known to do if you'd taken the time to read the instructions). You cover your head with your hands as the blender turns into

60

something resembling an erupting volcano and blows two cups of self-rising flour, half a teaspoon of baking soda, a quarter teaspoon of salt, half a cup of cocoa, one cup of sugar, $1\frac{1}{4}$ sticks of butter, one cup of milk, one teaspoon of vanilla extract, and two eggs all over the kitchen. Only it seems like a lot more. You switch the blender off.

*If you run away, go to 10.
*If you try to clean up the mess, go to 11.

10

You run out of the house and down the street in a blind panic. You mom is going to KILL you when she sees what you've done to the kitchen. You run and run and run, not looking — or caring — where you're going. Eventually, many hours later, you stop, exhausted, panting, delirious, and realize that you are completely lost. But luck is on your side. You are discovered by a gang of bank robbers. They take you in and look after you. All they ask in return is

that you become the driver of their getaway car and although you know that bank robbing is against the law, you are so grateful to them that you agree. On your very first job, as you pull away from the curb, tires screeching, you remember that you can't drive and your car goes skidding out of control head-on into a tanker carrying an enormous payload of $C_3H_5N_3O_9$. Nitroglycerine! But luck is still on your side. Miraculously, the truck doesn't explode. You and your passengers get out of the car, unhurt. But the police are chasing you. You run — straight into the path of an old lady in a motorized wheelchair. Your luck runs out. You trip and fall down and she runs over your head. You die.

THE END

11

You scrape the ingredients off the ceiling, the walls, the counters, and the floor — where your dog, Sooty, is busily licking up everything he can. He vomits. You shoo Sooty out of the kitchen. He gets back in and eats his vomit. Then he vomits it back up again. You shoo him out again. When you're sure he has gone, you pour as much of the retrieved ingredients as possible into the lightly greased cake pan, set the timer for 60 minutes, and place the cake in the oven.

*If the oven is not giving off any heat, go to 12.
*If the oven is giving off heat, but you're wondering why the cake is making a scratching and whining noise, go to 13.

12

You idiot! You turned the gas on, but you forgot to light it. You get a match. You strike it, completely unaware that in the meantime, the whole kitchen has filled up with gas. *KABOOM!* The oven explodes. The kitchen explodes. You explode. You die.

THE END

13

You kneel down and look through the oven door window. It's not the cake making a scratching and whining noise. It's Sooty! He must have snuck in there when you weren't looking. You open the oven door and stand back as he charges out of the oven and runs around the kitchen with his tail on fire.

*If Sooty is going crazy and his tail brushes against you, go to 14.
*If Sooty is going crazy and his tail brushes against the kitchen tablecloth, go to 15.

14

You say, "uh-oh," as your pants catch on fire. You rush to the sink to get some water to put yourself out but some of the chocolate cake ingredients are stuck in the faucet and have set like cement. The water can't get through. You burn. You die.

THE END

PHEW!

15

You say, "uh-oh," over and over again as you stare at the flaming tablecloth. You grab a dish towel and try to use it to smother the fire. But not like that, you idiot! Now look what you've done — you've set the dish towel on fire! You  drop it onto the floor and the linoleum starts melting. You try to turn on the kitchen faucet to get some water to put the tablecloth out, but some of the chocolate cake ingredients are stuck in the faucet and have set like cement. There's no water. You run to the nearest bathroom, but it's locked. Your sister, Jen, is in there taking a shower. She'll be in there a long  time. But the upstairs toilet is free. You go in, put your head in the bowl, and get a mouthful of toilet water. You run back to the kitchen and spit the water onto the burning tablecloth, dish towel, and floor.

*If you succeed in putting out the fire, but accidentally swallow some of the water, go to 16.
*If you succeed in putting out the fire and DON'T accidentally swallow some of the water, go to 17.

EVERYTHING'S BACK TO NORMAL.

16

You feel a little bit ill. No wonder. You just drank toilet water, you idiot! Dirty, filthy, stinking, horrible, disgusting toilet water that contains more than three billion deadly microbes per drop. The microbes enter your stomach. The microbes enter your bloodstream. You start to feel **REALLY** ill. You turn green. You turn blue. You turn an extraordinarily beautiful shade of purple. You die.

THE END

17

You check the cake. You check the dog. Sooty's tail is still on fire. You grab Sooty by the collar, pick him up, and run to the toilet. You try to plunge Sooty's backside into the bowl, but he thinks you're trying to give him a bath — and he hates taking a bath even more than he hates having his tail on fire. He stiffens his body and legs and won't let you push him in. As you struggle to push him into the

OOPS! SPOKE TOO SOON.

toilet, you grab the top of the toilet for support. At last you succeed. There's a great hiss and cloud of steam as Sooty's flaming tail hits the water. But at the same time, you accidentally lean on the handle and the toilet flushes.

*If you manage to hold on to Sooty despite the power of the flush, go to 18.
*If Sooty gets flushed away, go to 19.

18

You pull Sooty out of the toilet and turn around. AAAGGHHH! It's your mother! And she's caught you red-handed, having apparently just tried to flush the dog down the toilet. She loves Sooty and has often said that if she ever catches you — or anyone else — doing anything cruel to him, she will kill you. And picking up the toilet brush in one hand and a can of air freshener in the other, she proves to be as good as her word. You die.

THE END

GOLLY, LEGS! THAT'S NICE.

Oh no! You just flushed Sooty down the toilet. Your mother loves Sooty and has often said that if she ever catches you — or anyone else — doing anything cruel to him, she will kill you. And you know that she's not joking. You have to get him back. You put one foot into the toilet. You put the other foot into the toilet. You press the handle and next thing you know you're whooshing at high speed down the S-bend and out along the pipes. It's just like a waterslide, except it's much longer and much smellier. You go through the sewer lines and then you end up in the open sea. No sign of Sooty . . . You're weak and tired. . . . You're going under, but then you see a whale.

*If the whale ignores you, go to 20.
*If the whale swallows you, go to 21.

A LITTLE TOO BIG, MAYBE!

68

20

The whale ignores you . . . but the shark behind it doesn't. It bites you in half. You die.

THE END

21

You go down into the whale's stomach. You find Sooty! You tickle the whale's tonsils. The whale sneezes. You and Sooty are blown out of the top of the whale's head — so hard that you fly out over the ocean and over the land and, despite the odds against it, you go flying down the chimney of your house. Luckily, Sooty goes first and softens your fall. You're both a little dirty, but okay. You go into the kitchen. You check the cake. It's on fire. You take it out of the oven and carry it to the bathroom where you extinguish the flames by putting the cake in the toilet bowl (being very careful not to accidentally push the handle). You take the soggy cake out of the toilet and carry it back to the kitchen. You use a knife to scrape off the burned parts. You use a hammer and chisel to remove the REALLY burned parts. But it's not finished yet. You need to

STOP, LEGS!

decorate the cake. To make a simple and effective cake decoration, you need a Barbie doll. You go to Jen's bedroom to steal one from her collection.

*If Jen catches you stealing one of her Barbie dolls, go to 22.
*If you steal one of Jen's Barbie dolls without getting caught, go to 23.

22

You enter Jen's bedroom. You are almost overwhelmed by the stench of her perfume, but you manage to endure it for long enough to grab one of her Barbie dolls. But just as your hands close around Barbie's throat, you hear a noise behind you, and then hands close around YOUR throat. It's Jen. She reminds you that there is a sign on her bedroom door clearly stating that anybody who comes into the room without her permission will suffer total and utter annihilation. You nod. You suffer total and utter annihilation. You die.

THE END

You enter Jen's bedroom. You are almost overwhelmed by the stench of her perfume, but you manage to endure it for long enough to grab one of her Barbie dolls. You take the Barbie doll back to the kitchen, cut it in half, and shove it into the top of the cake. Then you use some icing to write "TO MOM, WITH LOVE FROM YOUR BEST AND FAVORITE CHILD, ANDY."

You walk up the stairs and into your mother's bedroom.

"Happy Mother's Day," you say. "I've got a surprise for you down in the kitchen."

She looks worried. "I'll be right down," she says.

You run back down to prepare the kitchen, but as you run back into the kitchen, you are definitely NOT prepared for what you see. Sooty is standing up on a chair at the kitchen table and is wolfing down the last bit of the chocolate cake that you have spent the whole morning making. You are furious. You grab Sooty by what's left of his tail, and throw him into the backyard, and lock the door. Not wasting a second, you run down to

UH-OH.

71

the store and buy a cake. When you get back, you steal another Barbie doll from Jen's bedroom, cut it in half, shove it into the top of the cake, whip up a new batch of icing, write a new message on the top of the cake, and put the cake on the table. It's beautiful. Perfect. You stand and admire the cake in awe.

Congratulations! You have chosen well. You don't know it, but you could have been electrocuted, bitten by a rat, had a bowling ball fall on top of your head, ground your fingers in the blender, and drowned in your own blood, been run over by an old lady in a motorized wheelchair, been killed in a gas oven explosion, burned, poisoned by toilet water, killed by your mother, bitten in half by a shark, or been totally and utterly annihilated by Jen. But you survived — despite the odds, you triumphed!

Your mom comes in. She's overwhelmed. She's crying. "Oh, Andy," she says, "that is the most beautiful cake anybody has ever made me."

"It's nothing special," you say. "I just wanted to say 'I love you.'"

ARRRGHH!

Your dad comes in. Jen comes in. They are impressed, as well. Everybody sits down and eats a piece. Big success.

You look out the window. You see Sooty lying in the backyard, his legs sticking up in the air. Uh-oh. He ate the first cake. What a stroke of luck that you didn't feed the family THAT cake. You hear a clunk behind you.  Followed by two more clunks. You turn back to the table. Your mom, your dad, and your sister are lying on their backs, their legs in the air. All dead. But how can that be? You BOUGHT that cake. It can't have been poisoned. It didn't have anything disgusting happen to it.

But then you remember the icing. The thing that both cakes had in common was the icing! You look at the ingredients on the counter. Uh-oh. Instead of icing sugar, you accidentally used the poison that your father was using to kill the rats.

"Oh well," you say, trying to look on the bright side. "At least I'm still alive."

But then the door bursts open and the police come in. They arrest you, take you  back to the station, and charge you with murder

by cake. And then you're tried and found guilty, and although your state no longer has the death penalty, they bring it back especially for you, and you're hanged by the neck until you're dead. You die.

THE END

TWO BROWN BLOBS

(THE MOST DISGUSTING THING THAT EVER HAPPENED TO ME IN MY WHOLE LIFE !!!)

By

ANDY GRIFFITHS (Age 4½)

with a ~~little~~ lot of help from

TERRY DENTON

(Age 6¾)

THE TWO BROWN BLOBS were starting to...

FREAK ME OUT!!

It was time to take serious evasive action.

S.O.S SURVIVAL GUIDE (bathtub version)

What to do if threatened by BLOBS.

I sucked my chest in,

made myself as skinny as I could,

grabbed my duck,

AND MOVED PAST THEM AS SLOWLY AND CAREFULLY + SILENTLY AS POSSIBLE, DOWN TO THE OTHER END OF THE TUB.

79

I ALWAYS WANTED TO BE A RUBBER DUCKY.

At last we could run no more...

My duck and I were tired...

...VERY tired.

It was time to take REALLY serious evasive action!

MOM!

But she didn't come... I tried again... even louder.

MOM!

81

I'M JUST A PEN LINE DUCKY.

I WAS RUNNING OUT OF OPTIONS...
I WAS DESPERATE...
I DECIDED TO TRY TALKING
TO THEM...

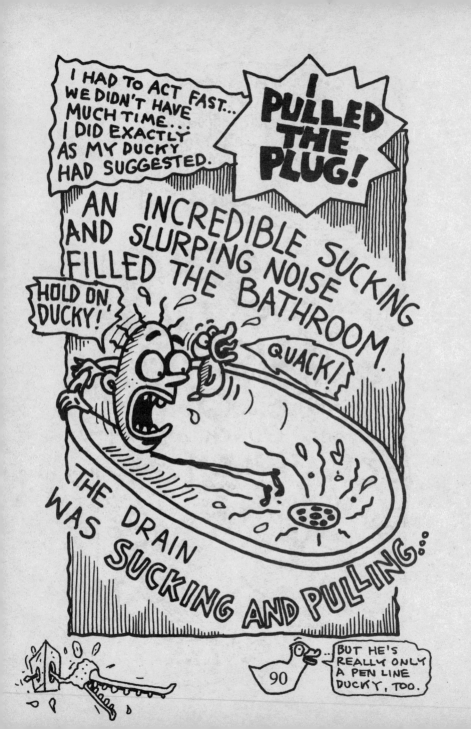

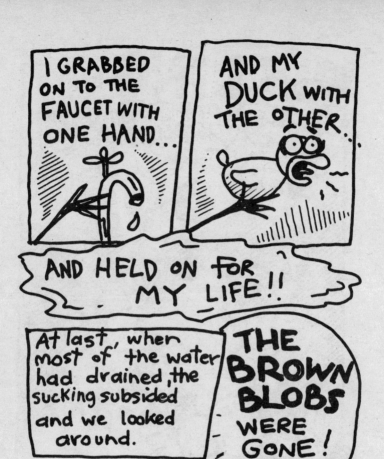

I GRABBED ON TO THE FAUCET WITH ONE HAND...

AND MY DUCK WITH THE OTHER...

AND HELD ON FOR MY LIFE!!

At last, when most of the water had drained, the sucking subsided and we looked around.

THE BROWN BLOBS WERE GONE!

They had been sucked down the drain along with the water.

92

AND HE GETS THE BEST LINES, TOO.

SHUT UP!

'm drinking some soda and I feel a really beautiful burp building up. I lean across to Jen.

"Jen," I say. "Want to hear a secret?"

I put my mouth right up to her ear and burp as loud as I can.

"You're disgusting!" says Jen. "Mom, Andy just burped in my ear."

"I know," sighs Mom. "I heard it."

"Hey!" I say. "You weren't supposed to be listening. It was a secret."

"Well, aren't you going to do anything?" Jen says to Mom.

Mom sighs again. "Just ignore him," she says.

"I CAN'T ignore him," says Jen. "He's filling up the camper with burp gas!"

QUEEN'S CHRISTMAS MESSAGE.

"I can't help it," I say, burping again. "It's the soda."

"Well, stop drinking it, then," says Jen.

"You're not the boss of the camper," I say. "You can't tell me what to do."

"Yes, I can," says Jen.

"No, you can't," I say.

"Why don't you just SHUT UP!?" she says.

"Why don't YOU shut up?" I say.

"Because I said it first," says Jen.

"So," I say. "I said it last."

Jen puts her fingers in her ears and starts yelling.

"SHUT UP!" she yells. "SHUT UP! SHUT UP! SHUT UP!"

I grab one of her hands and pull it away from her ear.

"YOU shut up," I say.

"Would you BOTH shut up?" says Dad. "I'm trying to read the newspaper!"

There is a loud clap of thunder, a flash of lightning, and then a fresh downpour of heavy rain.

This is the worst vacation we've ever been on.

We've been trapped in this camper for a week now, and it's rained every single day.

There is a burst of loud laughter from the camper next to us.

"Oh, great!" yells a shrill voice. "I just won second prize in a beauty contest!"

"The judges must have been blind!" says another voice, followed by more laughter.

"Shut up!" laughs the shrill voice.

They're playing Monopoly. Again. They play it all the time. When they're not playing Scrabble, that is. Or Trivial Pursuit. Or Twister. All they do is play games and have fun. They're really getting on my nerves.

"Hey, why don't WE play a game?" says Mom.

"We don't have any," says Jen. "Andy forgot to pack them. One simple job to do, and he couldn't even do that. Hopeless."

"Shut up," I say.

"YOU shut up," says Jen.

Another thunderclap rocks the camper.

"We can still play a game," says Mom. "How about I Spy?"

Jen groans.

ARE YOU LOOKING FOR THE EVEN MORE DISGUSTING THING FROM PAGE 18?

WELL, IT'S NOT HERE, JELL-O BRAIN! TRY PAGE 151.

97

I groan.

"What's wrong with I Spy?" says Mom.

"It's BORING," I say.

"But you used to love it!" says Mom.

"Yeah," I say, "when I was about two years old."

"Don't be silly," says Mom. "You couldn't even talk when you were two."

"Those were the days," says Dad from behind the newspaper.

Jen laughs.

"Shut up, Jen," I say.

"YOU shut up," says Jen.

"I spy with my little eye," says Mom loudly, "something beginning with *C*."

I look around. This will be easy. Mom's "I spies" are always so lame.

"Camper," I say.

"Very good, Andy," says Mom. "Got it in one."

"All right!" I say. "I win! I'm the winner! The best! The greatest! The champion! Did you hear that, Jen? I WON!"

Jen rolls her eyes. "Grow up!" she says.

"And you LOST," I say. "That makes ME better than YOU!"

"It does not," she says.

"Yes, it does!" I say.

"Just shut up," she says, "and take your turn."

"I spy with my little eye," I say, "something beginning with *S-L* — SORE LOSER."

"Tell him to shut up, Mom," says Jen.

"Andy," says Mom, "are you going to take your turn or not?"

"Yes," I say. "I spy with my little eye, something beginning with *E*."

The rain drums down hard on the roof while Jen and Mom look around the camper.

"Eggs?" says Jen, staring at the remains of our breakfast on the table.

"Sort of," I say, "but not quite."

"Egg cups?" says Mom.

"Sort of," I say, "but not quite."

"Eggshells?" says Jen.

"Hmmm," I say. "Sort of, but not quite."

"Egg carton?" says Mom.

"There is no egg carton," I say.

"There was, though," says Mom.

"Yes," I say, "but you can't see it now, can

you? Why would I say I can see something that I can't see?"

"It's never stopped you before," says Jen.

"Shut up," I say.

"You shut up," says Jen.

"Come on, you two," says Mom. "Don't spoil the fun."

There is another crack of thunder and the drumming on the roof gets louder.

Dad looks up from his newspaper.

"Is that hail?" he says.

I push back the little curtain and look out.

"No," I say. "Just more rain."

"Egghead," says Jen.

"Egghead?" I say. "I can't see an egghead."

"It's right there on top of your neck," says Jen.

"I do not have an egghead!" I say. "Do I, Mom?"

"Well," says Mom, studying my head closely. "It is a little oval-shaped, dear."

"IT IS NOT!" I say. "Anyway, it's not egghead! Can we move on?"

"We give up," says Jen.

"You can't give up," I say. "You only just started."

Jen sighs. "I bet this is a stupid one," she says. "Like 'air' or something."

I shake my head.

"It's not stupid," I say. "I promise."

"Well, it better not be," says Jen.

"Just guess," I say.

"Eyes," says Jen.

"No," I say. "How could it be eyes — that doesn't even start with *E*."

"Yes, it does," says Jen.

"It doesn't," I say. "It starts with *I*."

Jen laughs.

"Eyes!" she says. "E-Y-E-S."

Oops.

"Oh," I say. "I thought you said ice."

"You did not," says Jen. "You can't spell!"

"I can so," I say. "Can't I, Mom?"

"Well, dear," says Mom. "You're coming along really well, but you did only get one out of twenty on your last spelling test."

Jen starts chanting. "Andy can't spe-ell! Andy can't spe-ell!"

"Shut up," I say.

"YOU shut up!" says Jen.

WE APOLOGIZE. THE MESSAGE ON THE PREVIOUS PAGE SHOULD HAVE READ: DO NOT TOUCH THIS SPOT! (SO IT'S PROBABLY TOO LATE NOW.) (SORRY.)

101

"No, YOU shut up!" I say.

"Eyebrows," says Mom.

"No."

"Eyelashes," says Jen.

"No."

"Elephant?" says Mom.

AN ESCAPED
SLUG
(SEE Pg 150)

Poor Mom. She's really not very good at this game.

"No," I say. "How could it be elephant?"

"It could be an ectoplasmic elephant," says Jen.

"Now you're just being stupid," I say. "There's no such thing as an ectoplasmic elephant, and even if there was, I can't see one in here."

"Of course not, you moron," says Jen. "'Ectoplasmic' means 'like a ghost.' An ectoplasmic elephant would be invisible. So how could you see one, anyway?"

"No, Jen," I say. "If it's invisible, the question is how could YOU see it?"

"Because I'm psychic," says Jen.

"Oh, like a witch," I say. "That would explain the wart on the end of your nose."

"I don't have a wart on the end of my nose," says Jen.

WHY
ME?

"Oh, I'm sorry," I say. "That disgusting growth on your face IS your nose. My apologies."

"Shut up," says Jen.

"You shut up," I say.

"I give up," says Mom.

"Me, too," says Jen.

"What about you, Dad?" I say.

"He wasn't even playing," says Jen.

"Yeah, but he still has to give up."

"I gave up years ago," says Dad from behind the paper.

"All right then," I say. "Looks like I win again."

"What was the answer?" says Jen.

"Everything," I say.

"But that's stupid!" splutters Jen. "You can't just say 'everything.' You're supposed to do it in detail!"

"I did," I say. "Everything in the camper. How much more detail can you get?"

Jen looks like she's about to explode.

"I think I can spy something beginning with *S-L* again," I say.

"I spy with my little eye something beginning with *I*," she says. "Give up? Idiot!"

DANGER! THIS SPOT IS INFECTED WITH DISGUSTING BACTERIA... GUARANTEED TO START YOU FARTING, PUKING, BURPING, AND DRIBBLING! **DO NOT TOUCH!**

REX
STROMSKI
EXPLORES
CREATIVE
WAYS TO
SAY
SHUT UP!!

SHUT UP!

FROM INSIDE
A MILK CARTON

SHUT UP!

IN A
LIGHT-
BULB.

SHUT UP!

WHILE BEING
GRILLED AS
A KEBAB.

SHUT UP!

WHILE
PRETENDING
TO BE AN
INTERNATIONAL
SPACE
STATION.

There's another huge burst of laughter from the camper next door.

"Mom," I say. "Jen just called me an idiot."

"I did not," says Jen. "I didn't CALL him an idiot. I just said I could SEE an idiot."

"You were looking right at me when you said 'idiot,'" I say.

"I'm sure she didn't really mean it," says Mom.

"You always take her side," I say. "She's your favorite."

"No, she's not," says Mom.

"Oh good," I say, making a face at Jen. "Then that means I must be your favorite."

"No," says Mom. "I don't have a favorite. I love you both equally."

"Yeah," I say, "but if you had to choose, you'd choose ME wouldn't you?"

"But I don't have to choose," says Mom.

"But you'd choose me if you did," I say. "That's what you're saying isn't it?"

"I'm not saying anything of the sort," says Mom. "I'm just saying that I don't have to choose."

"Yeah," I say, "but what if you did?"

"But I don't," says Mom.

"But you might!" I say. "Just imagine that it's the middle of the night, right? And me and Jen are asleep in the camper. I'm at one end, and Jen's at the other."

"And in the middle there's a big cloud of your burp gas," says Jen.

"Shut up," I say.

"You shut up," she says.

"What's the point of this exactly, Andy?" says Mom.

"I'm just trying to find out, once and for all, which one of us is your favorite," I say. "Anyway, it's the middle of the night, and Jen and me are in the camper, and you and Dad have just come back. . . ."

"Where have we been?" says Mom.

"I don't know," I say. "You've been out . . . to a restaurant or something."

Mom frowns. "But we wouldn't go out and just leave you here alone."

"Yes we would," says Dad, rustling his paper. "In fact, let's do it right now."

"Very funny, Dad," I say, "but be serious for a moment — you've just come home and . . ."

"I'm sorry, Andy," says Mom, "but your father and I would not just go out and leave you both here alone. It would be irresponsible."

"Well, okay, you've taken the dirty clothes to the Laundromat."

"In the middle of the night?" says Mom.

"They're really dirty clothes," I say. "It's urgent."

"Oh, you mean like you wet the bed again and they have to wash the sheets?" says Jen.

"Shut up," I say.

"Why don't you shut up?" she says.

"Is there a point to this, Andy?" says Mom.

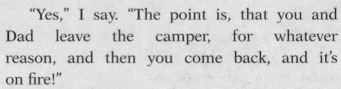

"Yes," I say. "The point is, that you and Dad leave the camper, for whatever reason, and then you come back, and it's on fire!"

"In the rain?" says Dad. "It would more likely be flooded."

"Just suppose the rain has stopped and the camper is on fire," I say.

"Why is it on fire?" says Mom.

"It just IS," I say.

"Probably all your burp gas," says Jen. "It's flammable, you know."

"Shut up about my burp gas," I say.

"YOU shut up," says Jen.

I reply with a deep, throaty belch. "You shut up . . ." I say, burping my words, "times infinity more than whatever you say!"

"You shut up times infinity to the power of ten," says Jen.

"You can't do that," I say.

"I just did!" says Jen.

"Infinity is infinite. It's already bigger than infinity to the power of ten," I say, "so I win."

"But I haven't shut up, have I?" says Jen. "So you lose."

She's got a point, but I'm not going to admit it. It's probably best to ignore her. She can be very immature.

A blast of heavy wind rocks the camper.

"Don't worry," I say. "It's probably just a tornado."

"I think you're right," says Jen. "Why don't you go outside and check?"

"Shut up!" I say.

"You shut up!" says Jen.

MR. SCRIBBLE'S NIGHT ADVENTURE

?

WHAT'S THAT NOISE?

WHERE'S MY FLASHLIGHT?

OUCH! I BUMPED MY HEAD!

WHERE IS MY FLASHLIGHT?

THIS STORY IS CONTINUED ON PAGE 242.

Dad clears his throat and lowers his newspaper. "Actually," he says, looking very serious, "I have a confession to make. I started the fire."

"What fire?" says Mom.

"The fire in the camper," says Dad.

"Why would you do a thing like that?" says Mom.

"Because I couldn't stand the bickering a moment longer," says Dad. "All I want to do is to read my newspaper in peace! Is that asking too much?"

"No," says Mom. "But you didn't have to burn the camper down!"

"Ignore him, Mom," I say. "The important thing is that you've come back to the camper —from wherever you were for whatever reason — and the camper is on fire — for whatever reason, it's not really important — and me and Jen are in the camper — me at one end and Jen at the other end. . . ."

"Don't forget the big cloud of burp gas in between," says Jen.

"Shut up," I say.

"You shut up," she says.

WHAT?

"And you've only got time to save one of us, right?" I say to Mom. "So, who would you save? Me — your great, wonderful, kind, generous, loving, irreplaceable son? Or Jen?"

Ha! I've got her now. She's going to have to choose! And who she chooses will reveal once and for all who her favorite child is, and maybe this whole stupid week trapped in a camper will have been some use after all.

Mom frowns. She bites her lip. "I've only got time to save one of you?" she says.

"Yes," I say.

"Just one question," she says.

"What is it?" I say.

"Where's Sooty?"

"Sooty?" I say. "He's not even here!"

"I know that," says Mom, "but if he were where would he be?"

"Probably on MY bed," I say. "After all, I AM his favorite."

"Are not," says Jen.

"Are so," I say.

"Andy just poked me, Mom," says Jen.

LIFE-CYCLE OF A CAMPER.

AT TWO MONTHS WHEELS START TO FORM.

NOW THE CAMPER IS READY TO GO OUT INTO THE WORLD ON ITS OWN.

"Shut up, Jen," says Mom. "I'm getting very tired of your constant whining."

Jen's eyes open wide. Her mouth is open wide, too. She is so shocked that she can hardly speak.

"Yeah," I say, smirking, "shut up, Jen."

"And you shut up, too, Andy," says Mom. "I'm trying to concentrate."

"Yeah," says Jen. "Shut up, Andy."

Mom shoots Jen a warning look.

"Sorry, Mom," I say, sticking my tongue out at Jen.

Mom stares at the roof of the camper.

"I think," she says, "all things considered, that I would save . . . Sooty."

"Huh?" I say. "You'd save the dog? Over one of us? But why?"

"Well," says Mom, "because Sooty is a poor, defenseless, innocent little animal. He doesn't deserve to die."

It's clear that Mom doesn't know Sooty very well. But that's beside the point.

"But what about ME?" I say. "I'm a poor, defenseless, innocent little boy. And I'm your son!"

"Don't be ridiculous," says Mom.

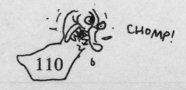

CHOMP!

"I'm not your son?" I say.

"We wish," says a muffled voice from behind the newspaper.

"I always KNEW you weren't REALLY my brother," says Jen. "I'm SO happy!"

"Shut up, Jen," I say.

"You shut up," she says. "Whoever you are!"

"Both of you shut up," says Mom. "I'm not saying you're not my son, Andy. I'm just saying you're not a poor, defenseless, innocent little boy. And Jen's not a poor, defenseless, innocent little girl. You both know where the door is. You could save yourselves. But Sooty might panic and not know what to do. So I'd save him."

"But while you're down at my end of the camper, you'd save me, too, wouldn't you?" I say.

"But you said I could only save one," she says. "And I can't carry both of you."

"But if you could, you'd save me, of course," I say. "Which settles the matter. I MUST be your favorite."

"I didn't say that," says Mom.

"So it must be ME," says Jen.

THE YOUNG CAMPER FIRST MUST CATCH A HOST CAR.

SOME CAMPERS WILL LOSE THEIR WHEELS...

AND DEVELOP INTO ADULT HOUSES.

OTHERS SIMPLY WANDER OFF INTO THE WILDERNESS TO DIE.

CHOMP! CHOMP

111

"I haven't said that, either," says Mom.

Now it's my turn to chant. "You're not Mom's fave-rit! You're not Mom's fave-rit!"

"Shut up," says Jen. "Neither are you."

"You shut up!" I say.

"Both of you shut up!" says Mom.

Suddenly, Dad jumps to his feet. "Shut up, all of you!" he says. "I'm trying to read the newspaper!!!"

"Why don't YOU shut up!" says Mom.

"HEY!" calls a voice from the next camper. "Why don't you ALL shut up in there!"

Dad jumps to his feet and jerks open the door. "I've got a better idea," he yells above the storm. "Why don't YOU loudmouths shut up instead?!"

"Don't you tell MY family to shut up," yells back the voice.

"Well, then, don't tell MY family to shut up!" yells Dad.

"Fine!" yells the voice. "How about YOU shut up, then!"

"I've got a better idea!" yells Dad. "How about YOU shut up ... TIMES INFINITY MORE THAN WHATEVER YOU SAY!"

There's no response from the other camper — they must know there's no use continuing the argument now that Dad's played the infinity card. Whoever it is, they're obviously a lot smarter than Jen.

"Good one, Dad!" I say.

Dad turns around.

"Shut up, Andy," he says quietly, and then he walks down the two little steps, out into the rain, still clutching his newspaper.

"Where are you going?" says Mom.

"To read my newspaper," says Dad. "In peace!"

"But it's pouring out there," says Mom.

"I'm well aware of that, dear," says Dad.

We watch Dad from the little rectangular window in the side of the camper. He walks to the playground in the middle of the RV park and sits down on one of the swings.

The rain is really coming down hard.

And it's starting to hail.

Within moments, Dad and his newspaper are soaked. But he doesn't seem to care. He just keeps sitting there, the paper getting wetter

and wetter, falling apart in his hands as he turns the pages.

"Is Dad all right, Mom?" I say.

"He's fine," says Mom. "He just needs a vacation, that's all."

"But we're already on vacation," says Jen.

"She means he needs a vacation from you, Jen," I say. "In fact, we all do."

"Shut up," says Jen.

"You shut up," I say.

Fun with Andy and Danny

Chapter 1:

FUN WITH A PUP

This is Andy.

Andy is a little boy.

This is Danny.

Danny is a little boy, too.

This is Sooty.

Sooty is a little pup.

Sooty can run.

Sooty can chase his tail.

Sooty runs around in circles chasing his tail.

Around and around and around.

Andy laughs.

He spins around.

"Look at me!" he says. "I am a pup!"

Danny spins around.

"Look at me!" he says. "I am a pup, too! Woof! Woof!"

The boys and the pup are all spinning around in circles.

They are spinning in circles in the middle of the living room.

They are laughing and spinning.

They are spinning so fast that they bump into each other.

Danny spins into a chair and falls over.

Crash!

Andy spins into the coffee table
and falls on his bottom.

Right on top of the pup.

Yelp!

The pup does not like being sat on.

"Oops," says Andy.

"Oops," says Danny.

The boys laugh.

They are having fun.

Fun with a pup.

Chapter 2:

FUN WITH A PUP AND A ROLL OF TOILET PAPER

This is Sooty.

This is Sooty's foot.

Sooty's foot is sore because Andy sat on it.

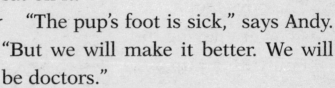

"The pup's foot is sick," says Andy. "But we will make it better. We will be doctors."

Dr. Danny and Dr. Andy put the pup in a cardboard box.

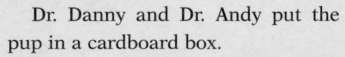

"This is the pup's bed," Dr. Andy says.

Dr. Danny gets Dr. Andy a roll of toilet paper. "This will make a good bandage," he says. "This will make the pup's foot better."

Dr. Danny wraps the pup's foot in toilet paper.

A IS FOR APPLE

But the pup does not like having its foot wrapped in toilet paper.

The pup jumps out of the box and runs out of the room, leaving a trail of toilet paper behind it.

"Stop that pup!" says Dr. Andy.

Dr. Danny runs after the pup.

Dr. Andy runs after the pup.

The boys chase the pup all over the house.

Up the stairs.

Down the stairs.

Along the hall.

In and out of the bedrooms.

There is toilet paper everywhere.

The boys see the toilet paper and laugh.

They have not caught the pup.

But they are having fun.

Fun with a pup and a roll of toilet paper.

B IS
FOR
BAT.

19

Chapter 3:
FUN WITH A ROLL
OF TOILET PAPER
AND A FAN

Andy and Danny are playing with toilet paper.

Andy is running around the room waving toilet paper in the air.

"Look at me!" he says. "I am an Olympic gymnast! I am going for gold!"

Danny laughs.

Danny wraps the toilet paper all around his body. He is walking with his arms straight out in front of him.

"Grrrrrrr!" he says. "I am a mummy! I am coming to eat your head!"

Andy squeals.

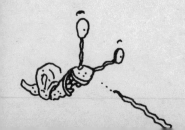

C IS
FOR
CAT!

120

Danny laughs.

Andy does not like that game.

Andy tears the toilet paper into little pieces and throws them up into the air.

"Look!" says Andy. "It is snowing!"

Danny laughs.

He rips up toilet paper, too.

The boys rip up all the toilet paper.

"I've got a good idea," says Andy. "I will get a fan. We can make a BLIZZARD!"

The boys use the fan to blow the snow all around the house.

"This is a very bad blizzard," says Andy. "I'm freezing! Brrrrrrr!"

The boys both laugh.

They are having fun.

Fun with a roll of toilet paper and a fan.

121

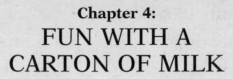

Chapter 4:
FUN WITH A CARTON OF MILK

The boys have had fun with a pup.

They have had fun with a roll of toilet paper.

They have had fun with a fan.

But all this fun has made the boys hungry.

"I am hungry," says Andy.

"Me, too," says Danny.

"Let's go to the kitchen and have some milk," says Andy.

The boys go to the kitchen.

Andy takes a carton of milk out of the fridge.

Danny takes two cups out of the cabinet and puts them on the counter.

Andy pours the milk into the cups.

122

E IS FOR EXPLOSION.

"That's not fair," says Danny. "You got more than me."

"No, I didn't," says Andy. "You already drank some."

"No, I didn't," says Danny.

"Yes, you did!" says Andy. "Look at your lip. You have a milk mustache!"

Andy laughs.

Danny gets mad. "Shut up," he says.

"No, YOU shut up," says Andy.

Danny throws his milk at Andy.

The milk goes all over Andy's face.

Danny laughs.

Andy gets mad. He throws his milk at Danny.

The milk goes all over Danny's face.

Andy laughs.

Danny picks up the carton and

F IS FOR FLAME.

pours the rest of the milk all over Andy's head.

The pup runs in and starts licking up the milk.

He looks up at the boys. The pup has a milk mustache.

The boys laugh.

They are having fun.

Fun with a carton of milk.

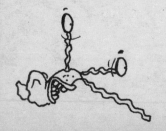

G IS FOR NOTHING PARTICULARLY INTERESTING SO FORGET G!

Chapter 5:
FUN WITH ANDY'S PARENTS

The boys are in the kitchen.

They are having fun with a carton of milk.

They hear the front door open.

"That's Mommy and Daddy," says Andy. "They have come home. Quick, let's hide."

"But where?" says Danny.

"Follow me!" says Andy. "I have a secret hiding place. They will never find us there."

The boys run to Andy's room and hide under his bed.

Andy's mommy and daddy come into the house.

They look in the living room.

"Oh dear!" says Mommy.

125

H IS FOR HEADACHE.

They look in the kitchen.

"Oh dear!" says Daddy.

They look all around the house.

"It looks like the boys have been having fun again," says Mommy.

"They won't be having much fun when I find them!" says Daddy.

The boys tremble with excitement under the bed.

Danny giggles. "I love hide-and-seek," he says.

Andy giggles. "Me, too," he says.

"Shush!" says Danny.

The footsteps are coming closer.

And closer.

And closer.

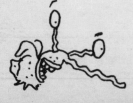

Andy and Danny clutch each other tightly.

They do not dare to breathe.

The boys are having fun.

Fun with Andy's parents.

Chapter 6:
FUN WITH A
VACUUM CLEANER

The boys have finished having fun with Andy's parents.

They are having NO FUN with a vacuum cleaner.

They have to suck up every last bit of toilet paper off the carpet.

And when they have finished that, they have to mop up the kitchen floor.

And when they have finished that, they have to straighten up the living room.

OR ELSE.

"Look at me!" says Andy, pointing the vacuum cleaner nozzle at Danny. "I am an alien. And this is my sucker-

J IS
FOR
JAM...
OR JAR...
OR JODHPURS!

upperer. And I am going to suck you up!" Danny squeals.

Andy laughs.

Danny grabs the nozzle and jabs it into Andy's stomach.

Andy squeals.

"Help! Help! He's sucking me up with his sucker-upperer! Help me somebody, please!"

Danny laughs.

Andy grabs the nozzle and points it at Danny's hair.

Danny squeals.

Andy laughs.

"Look at your hair, Danny," he says. "It's sticking up in the air!"

Danny looks in the mirror and laughs.

The boys are having fun after all.

Fun with a vacuum cleaner.

K IS ALSO FOR JODHPURS. I WISH I HAD A PAIR OF JODHPURS.

ANDY G'S

DEADFLY THEATER

PRESENTS . . .

A PLAY FOR DEAD FLIES

IN THREE ACTS

DEADFLYELLA

Please note: This play has been designed to be performed by the dead flies on my windowsill, but you don't need my dead flies . . . just look on any windowsill and you'll find plenty of your own. Collect them in a jar and pretty soon you'll have your own deadfly acting ensemble to delight and amuse your friends and family.

DEAD
FLY
NO. 1

CAST:

Deadflyella

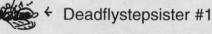 Deadflystepsister #1

Deadflystepsister #2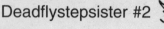

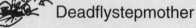 Deadflystepmother

Deadflygodmother

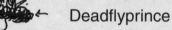 Deadflyprince

Deadflyprince's servant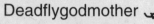

ACT I SCENE ONE

On a dusty windowsill, somewhere in any house.

DEADFLYELLA: *[using her proboscis as a vacuum cleaner]* Alas, poor me. Here I am working myself to the exoskeleton while my horrible stepsisters sit around on their fat little abdomens, laughing and enjoying themselves.

DEADFLYSTEPSISTER #1: Ha-ha!

DEADFLYSTEPSISTER #2: Hee-hee!

DEADFLYSTEPMOTHER: *[vomiting]*
BLEUGH! BLEUGH!

DEADFLYELLA: Oh, gross, deadfly puke!

DEADFLYSTEPSISTER #1: Well, don't just
stare at it, Deadflyella. Eat it up!

DEADFLYELLA: *[sucking it up with her
proboscis]* Alas, poor me.

DEADFLYSTEPSISTER #2: Oh well, we can't
sit around here all day watching
Deadflyella making a pig of herself. We
have to get ready for the Deadflyprince's
ball.

DEADFLYSTEPSISTER #1: Yes, we have to
make ourselves really beautiful.
Deadflyella, come here and shine my
wings.

DEADFLYSTEPSISTER #2: Brush my
bristles!

DEADFLYSTEPSISTER #1: Polish my large
compound eyes.

DEADFLYSTEPSISTER #2: Powder my
proboscis!

131

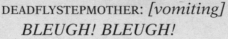

DEADFLYSTEPMOTHER: *[vomiting]*
 BLEUGH! BLEUGH!

DEADFLYELLA: Oh, gross, deadfly puke!

DEADFLYSTEPSISTERS: Well, don't just stare at it,
 Deadflyella. Eat it up!

DEADFLYELLA: But I can't. I have to get ready
 for the Deadflyprince's ball, too.

DEADFLYSTEPSISTER #1: You? That's a laugh!

DEADFLYSTEPSISTER #2: I'll say. As if!

DEADFLYSTEPMOTHER: *[vomiting] BLEUGH!*
 BLEUGH! BLEUGH!

ALL: Oh, gross!

DEADFLYSTEPSISTER #1: Now look what
 you've done, Deadflyella. You've made
 Deadflystepmother laugh so hard she's
 been sick.

DEADFLYSTEPSISTER #2: You'd better start
 sucking, Deadflyella! It will take you all
 night to get rid of all that.

DEADFLYELLA: *[sucking it up with her
 proboscis]* Alas, poor me.

HEE-
HEE

132

Later that night, on the same windowsill.

DEADFLYELLA: *[still sucking up Deadflystepmother's puke]* Oh, boo-hoo. I wish I could go to the ball, but I'll never get all this sucked up in time. And even if I could, I couldn't possibly go in this state. I've got deadfly puke all over me.

[There is a sudden puff of windowsill dust, and Deadflygodmother appears.]

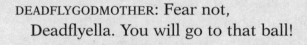

DEADFLYGODMOTHER: Fear not, Deadflyella. You will go to that ball!

DEADFLYELLA: What? Who are you?

DEADFLYGODMOTHER: I am your deadflygodmother, and I am here to grant your wish.

DEADFLYELLA: To be a ballerina?

DEADFLYGODMOTHER: Don't be ridiculous, child. Not that wish. Your other one. To go to the Deadflyprince's ball. Hurry, there isn't much time!

133

DEADFLYELLA: I can't. Look at all the deadfly puke I haven't sucked up yet. And look at me — I'm covered in it!

DEADFLYGODMOTHER: No problem. With my magic proboscis I'll have you ready in no time!

DEAD FLY N°. 11

[She touches Deadflyella with her proboscis.]

DEADFLYELLA: *[overcome]* Oh! Look at my shining wings, brushed bristles, polished compound eyeballs, powdered proboscis, V6 sports 200 HP 24-valve quad-cam thorax, and six little slippers made out of fresh dog poo! I'm so beautiful and desirable, I just can't believe it.

DEADFLYGODMOTHER: Yes, but it will only last until midnight. After that, you'll be just like you were before: a sad, dirty little deadfly covered in puke. Now don't forget. You must leave the ball before midnight.

DEADFLYELLA: *[taking off]* I will remember . . . thank you!

134

ACT II SCENE ONE

The same windowsill, a bit farther up.

DEADFLYSTEPSISTER #1: What a perfectly divine ball. I've never seen so many deadflies on the windowsill.

DEADFLYSTEPSISTER #2: Me neither. Would you care for some ratspew dip? It's delicious!

DEADFLYSTEPSISTER #1: Why, thank you. *[She giggles and points.]* Look who's coming! It's the prince! He's probably going to ask me to dance.

DEADFLYSTEPSISTER #2: No, he's probably going to ask ME to dance.

DEADFLYPRINCE: Greetings, deadflysisters. I wonder if I might ask of you a favor?

DEADFLYSTEPSISTER #1: *[jumping forward]* Yes, I'd be happy to dance with you, your deadflyness!

DEADFLYSTEPSISTER #2: *[jumping in front of Deadflystepsister #1]* ME FIRST!

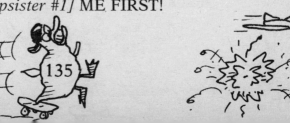

135

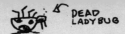

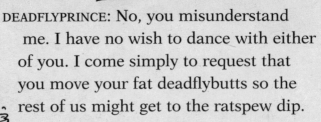

DEADFLYPRINCE: No, you misunderstand me. I have no wish to dance with either of you. I come simply to request that you move your fat deadflybutts so the rest of us might get to the ratspew dip.

DEADFLYSTEPSISTER #1: *[disappointed]* Yes, your deadflyness.

DEADFLYSTEPSISTER #2: I suppose a dance is out of the question?

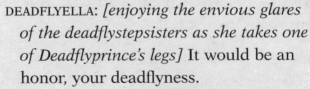

DEADFLYPRINCE: Yes.

[Suddenly there is a commotion as Deadflyella enters the ball.]

DEADFLYPRINCE: I say . . . who is that deadfly? Methinks she is the most beautiful deadfly I have ever seen. I simply MUST dance with her! *[He approaches Deadflyella.]* Excuse me . . . may I have the next dance?

DEADFLYELLA: *[enjoying the envious glares of the deadflystepsisters as she takes one of Deadflyprince's legs]* It would be an honor, your deadflyness.

136

DEAD MOSQUITO

DEADFLYPRINCE: Methinks you dance
divinely.

DEADFLYELLA: Methinks so, too.

DEADFLYPRINCE: What beautiful
compound eyes you have.

DEADFLYELLA: All the better to see all
eight thousand of you with.

DEADFLYPRINCE: What a beautiful
proboscis you have.

DEADFLYELLA: All the better to suck and
spray deadfly puke with.

DEADFLYPRINCE: What beautiful dog-poo
slippers you have. They look so moist.
They smell so fresh.

DEADFLYELLA: All the better to dance with
you with.

DEADFLYPRINCE: Methinks that last
sentence was a little confusing.

DEADFLYELLA: Please excuse me, but I'm a
little nervous. I've never danced with a
prince before.

137

[In the background a clock chimes midnight.]

DEADFLYELLA: What's that noise?

DEADFLYPRINCE: Just the clock striking midnight.

DEADFLYELLA: *[tearing herself out of Deadflyprince's six-legged embrace]* I have to fly.

DEADFLYPRINCE: No, come back!

DEADFLYELLA: Sorry, I can't! I have an urgent dentist's appointment.

DEADFLYPRINCE: But you don't have any teeth. *[As Deadflyella flies off, one of her dog-poo slippers slips off her foot and falls on Deadflyprince's head. He takes it off his head and holds it up.]* Come back. You forgot this!

[Deadflyprince's servant approaches.]

DEADFLYPRINCE'S SERVANT: It's no use, your deadflyness. She's gone.

DEADFLYPRINCE: Alas, poor me. She is the first deadfly that I have ever truly loved.

Methinks tomorrow we will search every windowsill in the house for the deadfly whose foot fits this slipper, and when we have found her I shall make her my deadfly bride.

  ACT III SCENE ONE

Still on the original windowsill, somewhere in the house.

DEADFLYELLA: Alas, poor me. Here I am working myself to the exoskeleton while my horrible deadflystepsisters sit around discussing last night's ball.

DEADFLYSTEPSISTER #1: Who WAS that blow-in with the dog-poo slippers, anyway?

DEADFLYSTEPSISTER #2: I have no idea, but she sure had some nerve. The prince was just about to ask me to dance when she came in. If I ever see her again, I'm going to give her a face full of germs!

DEADFLYSTEPMOTHER: *[vomiting]*
BLEUGH! BLEUGH!

DEADFLYELLA: Oh, gross, deadfly puke!

DEADFLYSTEPSISTER #1: Well, don't just stare at it, Deadflyella. Eat it up!

DEADFLYELLA: *[sucking it up with her proboscis]* Alas, poor me.

[There is a loud buzzing noise. Enter Deadflyprince and Deadflyprince's servant.]

DEADFLYPRINCE'S SERVANT: HEAR YE! HEAR YE!

DEADFLYSTEPSISTER #2: Stop shouting, we're not deaf.

DEADFLYPRINCE'S SERVANT: Sorry. Hear ye! Hear ye! Whosoever's foot fits the dog-poo slipper will be Deadflyprince's bride!

DEADFLYSTEPSISTER #1: What did he say? I couldn't hear a word.

DEADFLYSTEPSISTER #2: Me neither. Buzz a bit louder!

DEADFLYPRINCE'S SERVANT: I said, Hear ye! Hear ye! Whosoever's foot fits the dog-poo slipper will be Deadflyprince's bride!

UH. OH

DEADFLYSTEPSISTER #1: ME FIRST!

DEADFLYSTEPSISTER #2: *[shoving Deadflystepsister #1 out of the way]* NO, ME FIRST!

[They slip in Deadflystepmother's puke and fall over.]

DEADFLYPRINCE: *[aside]* Methinks these are two of the most putrescent daughters of maggots I have ever had the misfortune to lay my compound eyes upon — even before they slipped in yon deadfly puke.

DEADFLYSTEPSISTERS: Now look what you've made us do, Deadflyella!

DEADFLYELLA: It wasn't my fault.

DEADFLYSTEPSISTER #1: Shut up and pass me the slipper.

[Deadflyella takes the slipper from the servant and hands it to Deadflystepsister #1. She tries to force it onto one of her feet.]

DEADFLYSTEPSISTER #1: I can't do it . . . it must have shrunk!

DEADFLYSTEPSISTER #2: Here, give it to me! *[She snatches it off Deadflystepsister #1 and also tries to force it onto each of her feet, but with no luck.]* That's strange . . . they fit me perfectly last night.

DEADFLYSTEPMOTHER: *[vomiting all over the slipper]* BLEUGH! BLEUGH!

HALF DEAD FLY No. 19

ALL: Oh, gross, deadfly puke!

DEADFLYSTEPSISTER #1: Well, don't just stare at it, Deadflyella. Eat it up!

DEADFLYELLA: But I haven't tried on the dog-poo slipper yet!

DEADFLYSTEPSISTER #1: You? But you're just a stupid ugly deadfly covered in deadfly puke. Besides, you didn't even go to the ball.

DEAD FLY LEG

DEADFLYPRINCE'S SERVANT: She still has to try on the slipper. Orders is orders.

[Hands Deadflyella the slipper. She sucks the deadfly puke off the slipper and puts it onto one of her feet. The slipper fits perfectly.]

DEADFLYPRINCE: *[looking deep into Deadflyella's compound eyes]* Methinks it's a perfect fit! My love, will thou marry me?

DEADFLYELLA: *[looking deep into Deadflyprince's compound eyes]* Yes, of course. *[Aside]* Basically, I'd do anything to get off this filthy deadfly puke–covered windowsill.

DEADFLYPRINCE: *[again looking deep into Deadflyella's compound eyes]* You've made me the happiest deadfly in the world. Come, live with me near the toilet on the highest windowsill in the house. Together, methinks we will make beautiful maggots.

DEADFLYSTEPMOTHER: *[vomiting]* *BLEUGH! BLEUGH!*

DEADFLYPRINCE: Oh, gross — methinks I'm going to be sick. *[Vomiting] BLEUGH! BLEUGH!* Yep, methinks I was right.

DEADFLYPRINCE'S SERVANT: Double gross! Two piles of deadfly puke. Methinks I'm

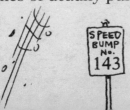

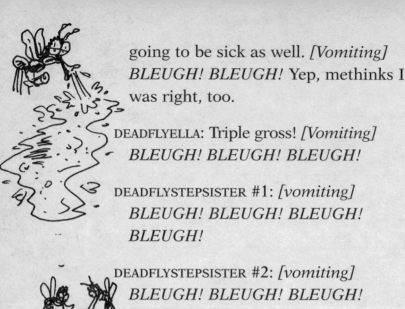

going to be sick as well. *[Vomiting]*
BLEUGH! BLEUGH! Yep, methinks I
was right, too.

DEADFLYELLA: Triple gross! *[Vomiting]*
BLEUGH! BLEUGH! BLEUGH!

DEADFLYSTEPSISTER #1: *[vomiting]*
BLEUGH! BLEUGH! BLEUGH!
BLEUGH!

DEADFLYSTEPSISTER #2: *[vomiting]*
BLEUGH! BLEUGH! BLEUGH!
BLEUGH! BLEUGH!

DEADFLYSTEPMOTHER: *[spurred on by all
the general bleughing]* BLEUGH!
BLEUGH! BLEUGH! BLEUGH!
BLEUGH! BLEUGH! BLEUGH!
BLEUGH! BLEUGH! BLEUGH!
BLEUGH! BLEUGH! BLEUGH!
BLEUGH! BLEUGH! BLEUGH!
BLEUGH! BLEUGH! BLEUGH!
BLEUGH! BLEUGH! BLEUGH!
BLEUGH! BLEUGH! BLEUGH!
BLEUGH! BLEUGH! BLEUGH!

DEAD
FLY
No.
20

SPLAT!!

144

DEADFLYELLA: *[to the deadflystepsisters]*
Well, don't just stare at it, you two. Eat
it up! *[Vomiting] BLEUGH! [She exits
with Deadflyprince and Deadflyprince's
servant.]*

DEADFLYSTEPSISTER #1: Alas, poor us.
[Vomiting] BLEUGH!

DEADFLYSTEPSISTER #2: Alas. *[Vomiting]
BLEUGH! BLEUGH!*

THE END

P.S. No flies were harmed in the making of this play. They
were dead already when I found them. Except for one that
was moving its legs a little bit, but it was on its back and I
doubt that it had long to live, anyway.
P.P.S. The dead flies in this play are fictitious and any resem-
blance to real flies, living or dead, is purely coincidental, although, when you think about it, highly likely because all
flies look pretty much the same.

THE STORY OF THE VERY STUPID BOY AND THE VERY BIG SLUG

A SCI-FI MYSTERY ACTION THRILLER ADVENTURE ROMANCE NOVEL
BY ANDY GRIFFITHS

DEDICATED TO LISA MACKNEY

DANNY.
(STUPID
BOY.)
↓

CHAPTER 1

Once upon a time, there were two boys. One boy was very stupid. His name was Danny. The other boy was brave, handsome, strong, kind, generous, and extremely intelligent. His name was Andy.

One day, the very stupid boy went to visit Andy in his backyard.

"I've figured out what I'm going to do for my science project," said the stupid boy. "I'm going to create a SUPER SLUG!"

"A SUPER SLUG?" said Andy, looking up from the time machine that he was building out of nothing more than an old cardboard refrigerator box and a few odds and ends that he'd found in his dad's shed. (That's how incredibly intelligent this boy was . . . he could do things like that.)

"Yeah!" said Danny, with little drops of spit flying from his mouth as they always did when he got excited. "A SUPER slug. A really BIG slug. A slug bigger than any other slug in the whole world!"

"Hmmm . . ." said Andy, stroking his chin. "Are you sure that's a good idea? I happen to know quite a lot about slugs, and believe me, you don't want to mess around with them. Why don't you help me with my time machine instead? It's almost finished. We could take it for a spin."

"Yeah," said the very stupid boy. "We could go into the future and see me winning a Nobel Prize for my SUPER SLUG."

ANDY. (smart boy.)

ASK YOURSELF...

IS IT A GOOD IDEA TO BREED VERY BIG SLUGS?
For the answer turn to page XXVI. or page 23.

OH, LOOK. A SLUG.

Andy shook his head sadly at his very stupid friend's stupidity.

"Well," said Andy, "if I can't talk you out of it, then at least let me help you. Just in case something goes wrong."

"No way," said Danny. "You're just jealous! You can't stand the thought that my science project might be better than your stupid old cardboard-box time machine. You just want to muscle in and take all the glory for yourself. I'm going home now. Home to make my SUPER SLUG!"

"You'll be sorry!" said Andy.

CHAPTER 2

"No, I won't be," said Danny.

CHAPTER 3

"Yes, you will," said Andy.

CHAPTER 4

The next day at school, the very stupid boy was very excited. He was clutching a shoe box close to his chest.

"Bet you want to know what's in my

shoe box," he said to the handsome, ex-tremely intelligent boy whose name was Andy.

"Let me guess," said Andy. "A giant slug?"

"Got it in one," said Danny, opening the lid of the box.

Andy looked inside.

He was amazed.

There, sitting in the shoe box, was the biggest and most disgusting slug he had ever seen. It was at least as big as a sausage. Maybe even bigger.

"But how?" said Andy, gasping and gagging. "How did you do this?"

The very stupid boy tapped the side of his nose. "That's for me to know and you to find out," he said.

"What are you going to do with it?" said Andy.

"Scare girls," said Danny. "Watch this!"

CHAPTER 5

The stupid boy walked up to a group of girls.

"Look at my slug," he said, taking the lid off the shoe box.

149

"AAAAGGGHHHHH!" screamed the girls when they saw it.

"Get it away from me!" screamed one girl.

"I think I'm going to be sick!" screamed another.

"That's disgusting," said Lisa Mackney — a very beautiful girl who didn't seem at all worried by the giant slug. "Put it away, you stupid boy."

"Darn," said Danny. "It's not working. It's not big enough."

"Yes, it is," said Andy. "It's plenty big enough. It's cruel to keep such a big slug in such a small box. You should let it go."

"No way!" said the very stupid boy. "I'll just get a bigger box. I've got to make my slug a lot bigger than this."

"You're being very stupid, Danny," said Andy. "You're messing with forces that you don't understand!"

"You're just jealous," said Danny, who was an ugly and stupid boy. "You just don't want my slug to beat your stupid cardboard-box time machine."

"That's not true, Danny," said Andy. "Listen to me. I don't know how you got the

THERE WAS
SUPPOSED TO
BE A SLUG
HERE, BUT
IT HAS
ESCAPED TO
SOMEWHERE
ELSE IN
THIS BOOK.
(HOW
ANNOYING!)

150

slug this big, but if you don't stop now, you'll be sorry."

CHAPTER 6

"No, I won't," said Danny as he marched away, clutching his shoe box close to his chest.

CHAPTER 7

"Yes, you will," said Andy, shaking his head at Danny's stupidity.

CHAPTER 8

Over the next few days, Andy worked on his time machine and hoped that Danny — who was a very stupid boy — had come to his senses and given up his stupid idea to make his gigantic slug even bigger. But then one afternoon, the phone rang.

CHAPTER 9

Brrrring brrrring! rang the telephone. *Brrrring brrrring!*

CHAPTER 10

Andy, who was in the middle of screwing the grinoolyscope (which he'd made out of a fork)

THE EVEN MORE DISGUSTING THING FROM PAGE 97 IS HERE

(DON'T LOOK.)

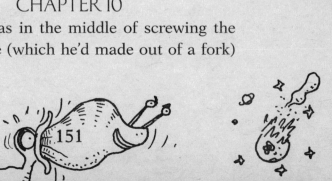

151

to the perambulic merimbulator (which he'd
made out of a soda can and a mattress spring),
picked up the telephone.

CHAPTER 11

"Hello?" said Andy.

CHAPTER 12

"Andy!" said a breathless, very stupid voice on
the other end of the telephone. "You've got to
help me! I'm in trouble!"

"What sort of trouble?" said Andy.

"BIG trouble!" said Danny. "Can you come
over here now? I don't have much time!"

"This wouldn't have anything to do with the
SUPER SLUG, would it?" said Andy.

"AAAAAAAAGGGGHHHHHHH!" screamed
Danny. And then the phone line went
dead.

Andy, who — as well as being handsome
and intelligent — was a kind and compas-
sionate boy, got on his bike and rode as
fast as he could to the very stupid boy's
house.

CHAPTER 13

I knew something like this would happen, thought Andy to himself as he rode. *I knew that stupid boy was too stupid to do something like this on his own.*

CHAPTER 14

When Andy got to the very stupid boy's house, he heard terrified screams coming from the garage. He waded his way through hundreds and hundreds of empty cans of dog food.

So that's how he did it! thought Andy. *He's been feeding the slug dog food!*

At last, waist-high in cans, he reached the garage door and pushed it open. Then he saw the most disgusting, terrifying sight imaginable: a **SUPER SLUG**. An enormous slug whose slimy gray blubbery body seemed to fill the entire garage.

"Danny? Where are you?" called Andy.

"I'm here," called Danny. "Underneath the workbench. Help me!"

"How?" said Andy.

"Use the pitchfork!" said Danny.

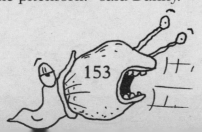

153

Andy looked around. There was a pitchfork leaning up against the garage wall. Although he was a very kind boy, and hated to see — or to be — the cause of any animal's suffering, he picked up the pitchfork and drove it deep into the slug's hide. Or belly. Or shoulder. Or whatever part of it it was. (It's hard to tell with a slug.) But the slug hardly reacted at all. Andy pulled the pitchfork out and plunged it into the slug over and over again. With each plunge, great geysers of slug slime spurted out of the slug, but if the slug was worried, it certainly wasn't showing it.

"Hurry up," called Danny. "It's trying to eat me!"

"I can't kill it!" said Andy, who was completely covered in slug slime. "It's indestructible!"

But luckily Andy, who was not only brave but also extremely intelligent, had a brilliant idea.

"Hang on, Danny," he yelled. "I'll be back!"

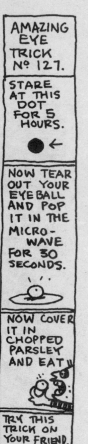

AMAZING EYE TRICK No. 127.

STARE AT THIS DOT FOR 5 HOURS.

● ←

NOW TEAR OUT YOUR EYE BALL AND POP IT IN THE MICRO-WAVE FOR 30 SECONDS.

NOW COVER IT IN CHOPPED PARSLEY AND EAT

TRY THIS TRICK ON YOUR FRIEND.

CHAPTER 15

Andy ran into the house and into the kitchen. He searched the shelves until he found what he was looking for.

CHAPTER 16

A salt shaker!

CHAPTER 17

Because Andy, who was not only brave and extremely intelligent but also very knowledgeable about slugs, knew that slugs HATE salt.

CHAPTER 18

Brilliant!

CHAPTER 19

Andy, who was not only brave, extremely intelligent, and very knowledgeable about slugs, but also a very fast runner, was back at the garage in a flash.

"Suck salt, slug!" he yelled as he shook the container at the massively mutated mollusk.

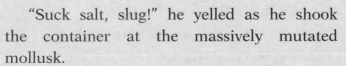

FAVORITE
SLUG
HIDING
PLACES
101.

BRILLIANT
SLUG
DISGUISES
1.

The great slug reared upward in pain, tearing though the metal roof of the garage as if it were no stronger than tissue paper.

"Quick, Danny," yelled Andy over the noise, "Get out while you can!"

Danny, the very stupid boy, darted out from underneath the bench and through the garage door just in time. The enormous slug crashed back down on top of the bench, crushing it to splinters.

Danny turned to Andy. "That could have been me," he said. "You saved my life."

Andy, who was not only brave, extremely intelligent, very knowledgeable about slugs, and a very fast runner, but also very modest, just shrugged.

"Don't mention it," he said.

As Andy spoke, the slug broke free of the garage and began sliding toward them.

"It's heading straight for us!" yelled Danny. "Stop it!"

"I can't!" said Andy, throwing the salt shaker at the slug. "I'm out of salt! Run!"

CHAPTER 20

The two boys ran as fast as they could (which, of course, was much faster for Andy than Danny, as Andy was such a fast runner).

CHAPTER 21

The slug, driven mad by the pain of the salt, chased after them.

NOTE: THE BRUSSELS SPROUT WHEELS.

CHAPTER 22

The two boys ran down the road, as fast as they could.

CHAPTER 23

The slug followed in hot pursuit, hydro-planing on a wave of slime.

CHAPTER 24

The police joined the chase. They shot at the slug with bullets, but the bullets didn't work. The slug just absorbed them and kept on going.

157

WELCOME TO PAGE 158.

CHAPTER 25

The army joined the chase. They fired heavy-duty mortar shells from their armored tanks, but the heavy-duty mortar shells didn't work. The slug just absorbed them and kept on going.

CHAPTER 26

The air force joined the chase. They dropped nuclear bombs right on top of the slug, but the nuclear bombs didn't work. The slug just absorbed them and kept on going.

CHAPTER 27

"IT'S NO USE!" yelled Andy, who, in addition to all his other talents, was also a qualified field operations commander. "YOU NEED TO USE SALT!"

PLEASE MOVE ON TO PAGE 159.

CHAPTER 28

The police started firing salt bullets at the slug. The army started firing heavy-duty salt shells at the slug. The air force dropped nuclear salt bombs on top of the slug. And the slug didn't like it one little bit. It let out a molluskian roar

158

of pain and disappeared inside an enormous quantity of slug foam.

"Hooray!" cheered the police.

"Hooray!" cheered the army.

"Hooray!"cheered the air force.

"Hooray!" cheered a large group of onlookers.

"Hooray!" cheered Danny.

"You're under arrest," a policeman said to Danny, the very stupid boy. "That was the most irresponsible science project in the history of the world."

"I tried to tell him that," said Andy, "but he wouldn't listen."

The policeman turned to Andy. "You're a hero, son," he said, "and the world owes a debt of gratitude to you."

"Thanks," said Andy, "but the battle isn't over yet."

"What are you talking about?" said the chief of police.

"The slug's not dead," said Andy. "It's just gone underground."

CHAPTER 29

Sure enough, as the bubbles subsided, it was just as Andy had predicted — there was no slug.

159

CATE AND ANNA DO THE GARDEN.

SPLAT!

THE END

Just an enormous hole in the ground where the slug had been.

"Quick!" yelled the police chief. "Fill in the hole!"

"Don't bother," said Andy. "It won't do any good. A slug as big as this will just keep eating and eating and eating. It won't be satisfied until it's eaten the whole world from the inside out."

"What can we do, then?" asked the chief of police. "Tell us."

"Nothing," said Andy. "There is nothing anybody can do. Danny's irresponsible science project is going to destroy the world."

CHAPTER 30

Sure enough, as Andy finished speaking, the ground seemed to bubble and boil and splinter into thousands of pieces underneath everybody's feet.

Many people were swallowed up into the cracks immediately. Cars, tanks, the police, the army, and the air force followed close behind.

All except for Andy, whose nimble feet and lightning reflexes ensured that he kept one step

ahead of the fragmenting ground. He had only one thought in his head.

"I have to get to my time machine, fast!"

CHAPTER 31

As Andy ran, he saw Lisa Mackney wandering dazed and confused amid the rubble.

"Andy!" she said. "What's happening?"

"It's Danny's fault!" said Andy. "His stupid SUPER SLUG is destroying the world!"

Lisa sighed. "Oh no," she said.

"Oh yes," said Andy, rolling his eyes. "I tried to warn him. But he wouldn't listen to me."

"What's going to happen, Andy?" said Lisa. Are we all doomed?"

"Not if I can help it," said Andy. "I have a time machine at my house. I haven't tested it yet, but I'm pretty sure it will work. If we can make it to the time machine, we can go back in time and stop Danny from creating his SUPER SLUG in the first place."

"But how?" said Lisa.

"We'll worry about that when we get there," said Andy. "Let's go!"

CHAPTER 32

SLUG
RODEO.

Andy and Lisa ran through the crumbling streets toward his house.

At last they arrived, panting hard.

"Wow!" said Lisa, staring at the time machine. "Very impressive! But where on earth did you get hold of a perambulic merimbulator?"

"I made it myself," said Andy. "I used a soda can and a mattress spring."

"Brilliant!" said Lisa, admiringly. "Utterly brilliant!"

"Let's just hope it works!" said Andy, modestly. He opened the door and ushered her in. "Step inside."

Andy followed Lisa into the machine and quickly began flicking switches and turning dials on the control panel. "Are you ready?"

"Yes," said Lisa. "Just a little scared."

"Hold my hand," said Andy, taking her hand in his. "Blast off!"

CHAPTER 33

"Nothing's happening," said Lisa.

OH, LOOK.
ANOTHER
YUMMY SLUG.

"It's already happened," said Andy. "If you open the door, you'll find we have returned to Earth exactly as it was one month ago, when Danny first got this whole stupid slug idea into his head."

SLUG MOON

Andy pushed open the door.

The time machine was suddenly flooded with sunlight.

Andy and Lisa stepped outside, and sure enough, they found Earth exactly as it had been one month ago. There was no marauding SUPER SLUG. No cracks in the ground. No disappearing houses.

JUST DISGUSTING!

"Wow!" said Lisa. "That's fantastic! But how do we find Danny before he does it all over again?"

"No problem," said Andy. "If my calculations are correct, he's just about to turn up."

"Here he is now!" said Lisa.

CHAPTER 34

Danny, who was a very stupid boy, walked into Andy's backyard.

"I've figured out what I'm going to do for my science project," he said. "I'm going to create a SUPER SLUG!"

MUST BE POLITE. DO YOU MIND IF I EAT YOU?

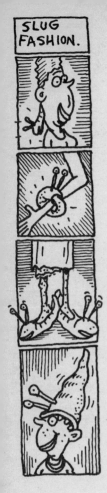

"A SUPER SLUG?" said Andy, smiling at Lisa.

"Yeah!" said Danny, with little drops of spit flying from his mouth as they always did when he got excited. "A SUPER slug. A really BIG slug. A slug bigger than any other slug in the whole world!"

"Hmmm . . ." said Andy, stroking his chin. "Are you sure that's a good idea? I happen to know quite a lot about slugs and, believe me, you don't want to mess around with them. Did I ever tell you THE STORY OF THE VERY STUPID BOY AND THE VERY BIG SLUG?"

"No," said Danny.

"Well," said Andy, winking at Lisa. "Once upon a time there were two boys . . ."

CHAPTER 35

"And that's how the world was destroyed," said Andy, looking at Danny, who was clearly terrified after hearing the story of the very stupid boy and the very big slug. "If only the very stupid boy had listened to the brave, handsome, strong, kind, generous, and extremely intelli-

OH, SURE.
GO AHEAD.

gent boy, then the whole tragedy could have been avoided."

"I . . . I . . . I don't think I'll make that SUPER SLUG after all," said Danny. "Can I help you with your time machine instead?"

"Of course, Danny!" said Andy, handing Danny an empty soda can with a mattress spring sticking out of the end. "How about you install the perambulic merimbulator?"

"Whatever you say, chief," said the very stupid boy.

CHAPTER 36

"You've done it!" whispered Lisa to Andy as Danny set to work. "You've saved the world!"

Andy shrugged modestly.

"It was nothing," he said. "It's certainly not the first time. And knowing Daniel Pickett, it probably won't be the last!"

THE END OF THE SCI-FI MYSTERY ACTION ADVENTURE ROMANCE NOVEL BY ANDY GRIFFITHS, WHICH WAS DEDICATED TO LISA MACKNEY.

MR. SCRIBBLE MEETS MR. PENCIL.

CAREFUL!

UH OH!

ARGH!!

SOMEBODY CALL AN AMBULANCE!

IS THIS THE END FOR MR. SCRIBBLE?

AFTER ALL, YOU'RE A DUCK AND I'M A SLUG.

BURP!

P.S. A perambulic merimbulator is the most important and complex component of a time machine. The difficulty of creating one has defeated all of the world's top scientists, but not Andy, who is not only brave, handsome, strong, kind, generous, extremely intelligent, very knowledgeable about slugs, a very fast runner, and very modest, but is also more brilliant than all of the world's top scientists put together.

About the Author

Andy Griffiths discovered a talent for disgusting his parents at an early age. Since then, he has gone on to disgust people all over the world with a truly disgusting array of disgusting noises, disgusting gestures, disgusting words, disgusting ideas, disgusting jokes, and disgusting stories. He has written four other titles in the Just! series — *Just Joking!, Just Annoying!, Just Stupid!,* and *Just Wacky!* — as well as the extremely disgusting novels, *The Day My Butt Went Psycho!* and *Zombie Butts from Uranus!*.

About the Illustrator

Terry Denton's disgusting life story.

etc., etc., blah, blah, blah, blah.

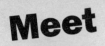
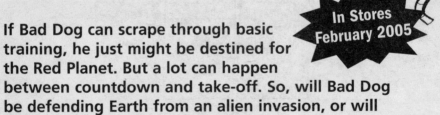

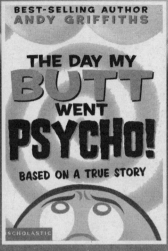
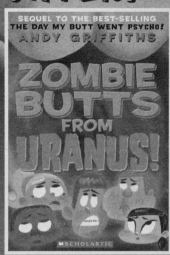

Kids from Alaska to Australia agree:
Andy Griffiths's JUST books are JUST great!